"Karen and I are going up the street to get an ice-cream cone."

"I like ice-cream cones."

"Got any money?"

"No."

Jill dug into her pocket to count what she had left. "Karen — do you have any extra?"

"No."

Jill looked up. Karen's voice was flat. "I'm not paying for her," she said.

"Oh . . . er. . . ." Jill shuffled the coins in her hand. "It's okay. I've got enough."

"I'm not going into Charlie's with her," Karen said. She spoke as if Dede wasn't even there. The words hung between them like skywriting in the air.

"Well . . . but . . . she walked here with me. . . ." Jill glanced at Dede She was staring at the ground. Shoot! Jill thought. Dede being along is wrecking everything. but I can't just leave her here on Main. You'd think Karen could see that! Why was she making such a big deal out of it, anyway?

**Other Apple paperbacks
you will enjoy:**

Starting with Melodie
 by Susan Beth Pfeffer

The Trouble with Soap
 by Margery Cuyler

Starstruck
 by Marisa Gioffre

Friends Are Like That
 by Patricia Hermes

Adorable Sunday
 by Marlene Fanta Shyer

Truth or Dare
 by Susan Beth Pfeffer

BETWEEN FRIENDS

Sheila Garrigue

AN
APPLE
PAPERBACK

SCHOLASTIC INC.
New York Toronto London Auckland Sydney

For Paul

I want to express my deep gratitude to my friend, Marilyn Quinby, for her advice and encouragement. I should also like to acknowledge the enthusiastic help I was given by Marsha Bendavid of the Pinesbridge School, BOCES, Yorktown, NY, John Braune of the Margaret Chapman School, Hawthorne, NY, and Chris O'Shea and the seventh graders of the Westlake Middle School, Thornwood, NY. And my loving thanks to Mimi. — S.G.

ISBN 0-590-43528-0

12 11 10 9 8 7 6 5 4 3 2 1   9/8 0 1 2 3/9

One

"There's a place!" Jill threaded her way through the sunbathers at the York Falls town pool. Mom followed with the beach bag. "Now," Jill said, as they spread their towels on an empty patch of grass, "aren't you glad we came?"

"No. There's too much to do at the house. We shouldn't be wasting time here."

"It's not wasting time. We've been unpacking and putting stuff away ever since the weekend. Everyone has to have some time off once in a while."

"Okay. You're right," Mom said. She lay down and closed her eyes against the August sun. "This does feel good!"

Jill looked at the families sitting on the grass with their sandwiches, and the groups of teenagers playing cards under the trees. It was good to see people again. We must've moved on to the quietest street in York Falls, she thought.

She got up. "I'm going in the water." She strolled toward the pool, trying to look as if she belonged there. Who can I talk to? she thought. There were a couple of girls over to one side, throwing a frisbee. As she watched, the frisbee took a wild curve in her direction and she fielded it. "Here!" She sailed it back to them, but they didn't ask her to play.

She joined the line at the diving board and grinned at the kids jostling in front of her. "Is it a good board?" she asked.

"If you're a diver, forget it!" a redheaded boy said. "It's dead as a . . . yeow!" Another boy pushed him in.

"You're docked, Kelleher! You, too, Parker!" the lifeguard yelled. "Get over here!"

Shoot, Jill thought. Just when I was getting a conversation going. She dove in. The water exploded against her head and cooled her skin as she arrowed down to the bottom.

Climbing out, she sat on the edge and swung her feet, watching what was happening. Then she stared, fascinated, at a group down at the far end. Gross. Retards. "Gross." She clamped her hand over her mouth. People'd think she was a weirdo, talking to herself.

What're retards doing at the town pool? she

wondered. She didn't know they could swim — they didn't even have swim bubbles or kickboards or anything. There were about a dozen of them with a couple of counselors. Some were learning strokes and some were jumping in and swimming across. Funny seeing so many all together. You usually only saw them when they were out with their families. Once she'd seen a grown man holding his mother's hand to cross the street.

Jill looked over at Mom. She was lying flat as a shadow on the grass, asleep in the sun. She'll get another burn, Jill thought. I'd better wake her. But she didn't. She'd only start nagging about having to leave and it was too soon.

There was a pickup game going on in the ballfield beyond the fence. Jill walked over. Maybe she could get on one of the teams. The kids looked at her for a moment, standing there, then went back to their game. Jill joined a girl in a bikini who was watching on the sidelines. The left fielder dropped an easy one. I could've caught that, she thought, and when the inning ended, she yelled, "D'you need any more players?"

"No," the catcher yelled back.

"What's the score?" Jill asked the girl in the bikini.

"Who knows?"

"Looks like a pretty good game," Jill said.

The girl stared at her. "I guess. Baseball bores me," she said. She waved at the pitcher and strolled away.

"Oh."

It was hot standing there and Jill went back to the pool. She did a racing dive and swam underwater to the other side. It was a good dive — she'd been on the junior swim team in San Diego. Hey, she thought, suppose someone notices and asks me to join the team here! She came up and looked hopefully at the faces around the edge. But nobody said anything.

Well, the retards are having fun anyway, she thought. Okay for them. They all know each other. They haven't just moved to a new town.

She climbed out of the pool. I might as well write to Susan now, she thought. Nothing else is happening, that's for sure. She pulled her pad and pencil out of the beach bag.

Dear Susan,

We've been in York Falls for a week and so far it's Dullsville. Larry and Tom have gone camping with some guy at Dad's new office. Dad got sent upstate right away and it looks like he's only going to get home on weekends for a while.

Mom and I have done just about all the unpacking. The house is okay. There must've been a sale on brown paint a while back because the whole inside is brown. Mom says we have to do it over.

Massachusetts is sticky hot and the only place to cool off is the town pool, which is where we are right now. Nobody speaks to you here. I wish we were still in San Diego.

Write and tell me about what the gang's doing.

> *Love,*
> *Jill*

Mom's shoulders were turning red.

"Mom. Hey, Mom!"

Her mother lay there as if a steamroller had gone over her.

"Mom, you're getting a burn."

"Mmph . . ."

"Wake up. Your shoulders are red."

"Darn! I didn't mean to fall asleep. Put a little lotion on, would you, honey?"

Jill squeezed some lotion onto her fingers and began smoothing it over her mother's shoulders. The closest to a tan Mom ever got were big orange freckles sprinkled all over. But she always kept trying, lying out for hours as though some miracle were going to happen to turn her golden brown. Jill ran a track of gel down Mom's backbone. Sometimes she felt like the mother.

"Mom — there are retards in the pool. Look!"

"Don't stare at them, Jill. It's rude."

"Don't you think it's weird having them come to the pool with everyone else?"

"No." Her mother spoke shortly.

"They can swim, some of them."

"Can't we talk about something more cheerful?" Mom turned on her back. "I'll just do my front a bit," she said. "Vitamin D. Good for the baby."

You'd never imagine that Mom was going to have a baby. She was so skinny, every knob on her shoulders showed, even the pattern of her ribs. There wasn't a bulge anywhere to show where a baby might be, not even a little softness. Jill kept thinking, funny there should be a new baby coming eleven whole years after me. That's a long time between.

Dad had said bitterly, "Great timing!" when Mom told him. Jill could hear their muffled voices through the bedroom wall. ". . . out of work for three months . . . I can't handle . . ." You could just hear Mom, apologetic and fearful, as if she'd done something wrong. Why was he being so mean to her? It was his baby too.

Jill had stayed rigid on her bed. He wasn't being fair at all. ". . . going out!" Dad said, and the front door slammed. There was silence beyond the wall. Mom was still in there — maybe crying. Jill had wondered, should I go in? But she didn't want them to know she could hear through the wall and she stayed put.

A long time later, Dad had come home. Jill heard him down the hall. Everything was very quiet and then he and her mother were laughing softly together and it was all right again.

Two weeks later he'd come home with the news that he'd finally found another job as an auditor for an accounting firm and for better money than before. The only thing was, it was in Massachusetts.

"Watch out!" Jill looked up. A beach ball came rocketing toward them. It bounced and knocked over someone's soda can. "Hey!" a woman cried angrily.

Jill jumped up to catch the ball. A girl in a red bathing suit was chasing it. She ran clumsily, breathing hard through her open mouth. She stopped when she saw Jill and stood a little way away, waiting.

"Those mongols! Shouldn't be allowed here, upsetting everybody!" the woman yelled.

"Here," Jill called to the girl. She threw the ball carefully into her outstretched hands.

"Thank you." The girl's voice was low and kind of rough. She turned and walked back to her friends.

"You're welcome," Jill said.

As soon as the girl turned, Mom sat up. She

had a funny, stiff look on her face. "Let's get out of here," she said. She began stuffing the towels and lotion into the beach bag.

"It's still early. Why do we have to?"

"It's getting . . . too crowded," Mom said. "Anyway, we've got a good twenty-minute walk home and there's so much to do — we shouldn't waste a whole afternoon here."

"Oh, Mom . . ."

"I mean it. Don't give me a hard time, Jilly. Dad'll be coming home tonight and I want to be able to show him we've made some real headway while he's been gone. I'd like to get started on those porch chairs."

Jill picked up the beach bag. "That's right! I forgot it's Friday!"

Two

Jill and Mom pulled the saggy old porch chairs out on the grass.

"Get the paint, Jilly. It's on the kitchen counter. The brushes are there, too."

Jill walked back up to the house. It was so much taller than their house in San Diego — old-fashioned and a bit rundown. The paint was peeling and the shutters hung at crazy angles. But it had a high, narrow gable and was covered with wooden shingles shaped like seashells. And there were two floors. She liked that. There was a tree outside and she could lie on her bed and look the birds straight in the eye. Tom and Larry's room was next to hers and Mom and Dad were down the hall by the bathroom. The porch in front of the house was wide, with broad wooden steps leading up to it, so even on a rainy day you could be out in the fresh air.

The houses up and down the street all looked about the same. Each had a little yard in front, with a path and a fence and a gate, and the sidewalks were lined with big old trees.

"Maples," Dad had said. "They'll be a sight in the fall!" He looked really happy for the first time in quite a while. He'd grown up in the East. "Wait'll you see a New England fall! You kids living all your lives in California — you can't imagine!"

They nodded. "Sure, Dad," they said.

Jill found the paint and carried it outside.

"What time is Dad getting home?" she asked.

"Not much before ten. He's got a long way to come."

"Then these chairs might even be dry by the time he gets here."

They settled down to work. The late afternoon sun struck at their faces, even in the shade of the tree. A trickle of sweat tracked down Jill's chest under her T-shirt and she scrubbed at it impatiently — there'd always been a breeze in California.

"When're the boys coming back?" she asked. "They're getting out of all the work!"

"There'll be plenty left for them, don't you worry. They'll be home Sunday."

"I wish I could've gone camping."

"I know. I'm sorry there wasn't anything for you, Jilly. But it seemed such a great chance for them to make some friends."

"Well, I sure would like to get to know *someone* around here! Where is everybody? I haven't seen one girl on this whole street all the times I've been up and down it. And when I talked to a kid at the ballfield, she looked at me as if I were from Planet X or something!"

"We just have to be patient, honey. I've always heard people take a while in New England. But when they finally do make friends, they're good ones. It's hard in summer with people away. You'll find some friends when school starts, you'll see." She ran a finger down Jill's cheek. "Anyway, I'm glad you didn't go camping. I'd have looked pretty funny rattling around in this place all alone." She threw down her paint brush. "Ugh! This smell's getting to me." Sweat stood out on her upper lip and her face looked like putty. "I . . . I think I'll lie down for a while."

"Are you okay?"

"It's just the paint."

"Do you want me to keep going?"

"No. Put the stuff away. We'll finish tomorrow. Maybe it'll be cooler. Tell you what — why don't you walk down to Main and get a pizza for supper? I'll throw a salad together when you get back."

She got up and walked into the house. There was a heaviness to her these days, even though she was so skinny. In California, she'd been full of energy, laughing all the time. I guess she's missing her friends, too, Jill thought, as she pressed the lid onto the white paint and stuck the brushes in a can of turpentine.

In the kitchen, she took three dollar bills and some change from her mother's purse and headed for the door. Upstairs, Mom was retching in the bathroom. It sounded awful.

"Maybe I shouldn't go?" she called up the stairs. "Can I do anything for you?"

"No. Go ahead." Mom's voice was muffled.

Jill put on her sneakers. Air-conditioned, Dad had called them, laughing at the holes in the toes. She started down the street and, as she'd done yesterday, she tried guessing who lived in all the houses. Someone was playing one-handed piano in one of them and she stood on her toes to see who it was. A girl about sixteen. Too old. Outside another house, a battered red tricycle was lying on its side and she could hear a baby crying. An old man sat asleep in a rocker on a porch on the next block — his newspaper in his lap and his head thrown back. A big black cat blinked at her from the steps. She waggled her fingers at it, but it was too lazy to come to see her. She crossed another street onto the last block before Main.

"Hey! You girl! Come up here!"

Jill jumped. At first she couldn't see where the voice was coming from. Then, in the shadows at the back of a porch, she saw a hand beckoning, bony and white. Jill backed up and squinted into the dark beyond the steps. It was an old woman.

"Yes. You. Come up here a moment." The voice was raspy.

"Well . . . I . . ."

The voice softened. "Oh, I won't bite you, girl. Just for a minute. I want to ask you something."

"I have to go to the store . . ."

"I know, I know. I won't keep you."

Jill let herself in the gate and slowly climbed the porch steps. The old woman motioned her forward.

"What's your name?"

"Jill. Jill Harvey. I . . . we just moved in last weekend."

"So that's it. Thought I knew everybody around here." The old woman nodded, satisfied. "See everyone sooner or later from my porch. Want a glass of my lemonade?"

"Well, I don't . . ."

"It's all right. Won't poison you. You can pour me some, too. Hotter'n Hades today."

Jill poured the lemonade. As she went toward the old woman, something soft moved under

13

her foot. There was a yelp and whatever it was scuttled under the couch. "Oh!" she said, startled. "I'm sorry. I hope I didn't hurt . . ."

"That's Squeak. No sense at all. Always getting underfoot." The old woman sipped the lemonade and then set it down with a shaky old hand. "Name's Mrs. Lacey. Easy to remember on account of the lacy curtains in my parlor windows."

"Yes, ma'am."

"Now. You look like a good girl to me. I've watched you come down the street a time or two and I've taken to you. Do that sometimes. So I asked you up here to see if you'd like to tackle a little job for me. Sit down, girl." Mrs. Lacey patted the couch beside her. "It's Squeak. Got to do something about him. Don't like walking him in this heat. Makes my heart beat a mite too fast. So how'd you like to walk him a couple times a day for me? I'd pay a quarter a day."

"Okay."

"Good. Are you used to dogs? Do you have one at home?"

"No. We used to . . . Jess. He got killed by a car."

"Too bad! Animals and traffic don't mix. Well, Squeak's no trouble — stays right on the leash. Here — come out of there, Squeak!" Mrs. Lacey leaned down and hauled a small dog from under the couch. He was low to the ground and had longish blond hair and a tail like a plume that curled over his back. His face looked as if someone had put his hand against it and pushed.

"Oh, he's cute! What kind of dog is he?" Jill asked.

"Squeak's a Pekinese. We've lived together a long time, haven't we, Squeak? And before him, I had his mother. His leash hangs on that hook by the door and you can come once in the morning and once about this time of day and take him up and down the street. Good for him. He's gett'ng fat."

Jill squatted down and let the dog sniff at her hand, and then stroked him softly between his small round ears.

"I'll start tomorrow," she told Mrs. Lacey.

"Good. Do you live on Maple?"

"Yes. Number 94."

"I know it. Augusta Miller's place. Well, you have a pal next door, don't you?"

"I . . ."

"That Marla Burns lives at 96, doesn't she? Must be about your age."

Jill shook her head. "I don't think so. I haven't seen a girl there."

"Yes, she does. She and her mother. Mother's divorced. Oh . . . now I recall . . . Marla goes to her grandma's in August."

Jill leaned forward. "I thought I was the only girl around here."

"Bless you, no. Let me see . . . there's Connie Ward. She lives around the corner on Main. She'd be about the right age. And Karen McCluskey lives somewhere in the sixty block. Nancy Cohen — she plays the cello right nice — and her big sister Jean is learning piano, I hear. None in the Kelleher family — all boys . . . Can't think of any more at present, but that's a start."

"Thanks, Mrs. Lacey!" Jill got up. "I'd better be going. I have to get a pizza for supper. Thanks for everything." She hurried down the porch steps. "I'll come for Squeak in the morning."

Jill ran down the block to Main. It'd be fun to walk that little dog every day and she could use the money. Now she'd have something else to write Susan about.

The pizza parlor smelled good. Jill studied the list tacked up behind the counter. I'd love that combination, she thought. Wish it didn't cost so much . . . Sausage? Mom's pale face popped into her mind. Sausage might be tough for her to handle right now. Finally, she decided on half meatball and half cheese and fifteen minutes later was on her way home, the white box warm in her hands.

A car was parked outside her house, its rear

door open. Jill hurried up the block to see who'd come to visit. As she got to her gate, a woman backed out of the car hauling a big suitcase and bumped into her. Jill almost dropped the pizza.

"Oh!" the woman said. "Shoot — I'm sorry, honey. I didn't hear you coming up behind me. Is the pizza okay?"

"Yes, fine." Jill stared at the woman. She was middle-aged. She had hair a kind of silver color in a long pageboy and she was wearing a black-and-white striped pantsuit.

The woman clapped her hand to her head. "Oh, for heaven's sakes, do you live here?"

"Yes," Jill said.

"Then you're the new people . . . I mean . . . well, isn't that great . . ." She laughed. "You don't have a clue who I am, do you?"

"No."

"I'm Mrs. Burns, honey. I live next door to you. I'm sorry — I'll move my car. I didn't know anyone'd moved in yet. But this is *great* — I've a kid just about your age. Marla's twelve — she'll be tickled pink when she finds out you've moved here."

Jill grinned. Mrs. Burns was nice. "I'm Jill Harvey. I'm going to be twelve in October . . . Is Marla home yet?"

"No, hon. She's still at her grandma's. But she'll be back in time for school. Then you two'll have to get together."

The pizza was cooling off fast.

"I'd better go. Mom's waiting for the pizza."

"Okay. Bon appetito, as they say!" Mrs. Burns waved gaily and began dragging the suitcase toward her house.

"Who's that?" Mom asked, as she closed the front door. She was looking better.

"It's Mrs. Burns from next door. And Mom! She's got a kid my age. She's away at her grandmother's, but she'll be back for school."

"What's she like, Mrs. Burns?" Mom asked, putting the pizza into the oven to heat up again. "She certainly has wild colored hair . . ."

"Oh, she's nice, Mom. Really. Very friendly. I bet you'll like her." Jill started setting the kitchen table. "Hey, Mom, I forgot to tell you about Mrs. Lacey . . ."

"I wish Dad could've gotten home in time for supper," Jill said, clearing the plates. "They should let him come home for supper on Friday after being away all week."

"Companies don't care about things like that, honey. He has to put in a full day's work before he starts home. He's brand new there, remember." Mom glanced at the clock. "Should be home by ten." Her eyes were bright. "It's been a long week, hasn't it?"

"You can say that again! This house seems so . . . big, when he's not here."

"I know."

At eight-thirty, Jill jumped up from watching TV. "He's here!" She ran to the door. But it was only Mrs. Burns, driving off.

At nine-fifteen, she ran to the door again. "I was sure I heard him," she said, coming back into the living room. "It must've been the TV."

At twenty to ten, he came. He looked tired, but his face lit up as he walked in the door.

"It's good to be home," he said, pulling them both against him. "*So* good!"

They stood there together, none of them wanting to let go.

A family circle, Jill thought. This is what it means.

Three

Jill and Tom and Larry dodged around each other clearing the breakfast things into the dishwasher. As she'd done every Friday since they'd moved, it seemed, Mom sat at the kitchen table making lists.

"We're out of nearly all the staples," she said, scribbling. "Thank goodness your father'll be home tonight with the car." She read over another sheet of paper, then said, "Tom, I want you to mow the grass today. And Larry, the basement's full of cobwebs. Sweep it out and then straighten your room up. And do something about that slimy fish tank . . . the whole upstairs smells of it. Jill, I need you to help me scrape the old paint off in the baby's room. The boys can pick up the paint I ordered later to-day, then we can work on that room tomorrow."

Tom said, "Swap you cutting the grass for cleaning the basement, Lar. Plus I'll throw in fixing the kitchen shutter."

"No way!" Larry said. "I mowed last time and it took forever. Dad wants it trimmed around every bush."

"Come on, Lar . . ."

The house was back to normal, except for Dad being gone. Well, Jill thought, at least he'll be home tonight. Earlier than usual, he had promised. She wiped off the counters and said, "I'm going to walk Squeak now, before it gets too hot."

"Okay, hon." Mom poured herself another cup of coffee. "Tell Mrs. Lacey Dad and I will walk down and visit with her after supper tomorrow."

"Okay."

Jill and Squeak had worked out a pretty good routine over the last thirteen days. Squeak was always waiting for her — sitting at the top of the porch steps and watching for her to come down the street. By the time she let herself in the gate and climbed up to the porch, he was trembling from end to end with excitement. If Mrs. Lacey wasn't around, Jill just picked up the leash and they took off. They'd turn back up the street the way she'd come, go past her house for maybe six more blocks, then cross over and walk down the other side past the Cohen and McCluskey houses to Main. There they'd turn again and head home to Mrs. Lacey's. Jill always got Squeak a bowl of fresh water and by the time she let herself out the gate he'd already be curled up in his basket and there'd be just a tired wag of his tail to say goodbye.

Sometimes Jill could hear Mrs. Lacey fussing around inside the house. Sometimes she'd be outside, snoozing on the couch. And sometimes she'd beckon Jill over into the shade to try a ginger cookie or pour some of the tart lemonade from the pitcher on the table. It was good up there on Mrs. Lacey's porch. A lot of the time they'd just sit without saying much at all — they'd become friends enough for that. But other times, Mrs. Lacey was in a talking mood and then she told Jill about the families up and down the street, or how it'd been in York Falls in the old days, when there was iceboating on the river below the falls and a big town picnic every Fourth of July. And Jill told her about California and the orange tree in their garden.

Mom laughed when Jill told her Mrs. Lacey's stories about the neighbors and the town. "Mrs. Lacey did the whole family a favor when she gave you that job! I'll bet we know more about

York Falls than some people who've lived here all their lives!"

Now Squeak pulled her along the sidewalk, leash at full stretch. His tail waved from side to side like a metronome as he trotted forward on his stubby legs. Jill could hear Jean Cohen practicing the piano in her front room, and from an upstairs window came the deep notes of Nancy's cello. How could they stand two different tunes going at the same time? They must wear earplugs!

They got to the junction with Main and, this time, Jill turned the corner to look in the dime store window. School was starting soon — she'd have to get some pencils, maybe a notebook or two, and a folder. She had $3.25 from Mrs. Lacey put away in her top drawer and by tomorrow night it'd be $3.50. She could get one of the folders with pretty covers.

They turned back. As they passed the second house from the corner of Main and Maple, a big red dog jumped the fence and came up to them. He stopped short, his tail waving gently from side to side, and greeted Squeak, first touching his nose and then sniffing him thoroughly all the way around. The red dog looked a lot like Jess . . .

"Hi."

A girl stood at the top of the porch steps. She

was dumpy, with eyes that slanted. The back of her head was sort of flat. She started down the steps. "Hi," she said again. "That's my dog."

Jill thought, she looks like one of those retards at the pool. "Yeah?" she said.

"That's Barney. He's my dog."

"Oh. Er . . . he's a nice dog." Jill looked around. Suppose someone saw her talking to a retard. She pulled at Squeak's leash, but now it was his turn to sniff. "Come *on*, Squeak . . ."

"Barney l-likes him," the girl said. "What's your name?"

"Uh . . . Jill. *Squeak* . . . um, what's yours?"

"Dede."

"Uh-huh." Jill stroked Barney's broad head. His tongue lolled out happily. She scratched him under his chin and he stretched his neck for her, just the way Jess . . . Jill stooped quickly and hugged him, hiding her face against his solid warm body. After a moment, she felt an awkward pat on her shoulder. "Don't cry. B-Barney likes you."

"Dede?" A woman's voice called from the house. "Who're you talking to out there? Dede?"

Dede's mother came down the steps. "Who . . . oh. Hello. I'm Dede's mother."

"Er . . . I'm Jill . . . Jill Harvey. We moved in at 94. I was just passing by."

"Our name is Atkins. Well, now. How would

you like to come in for a while? I bet I can find some cookies . . ." Mrs. Atkins was smiling brightly.

"Oh, no, that's okay. I have to go now. I can't stay. I'm sorry. I have to take Squeak home to Mrs. Lacey's . . ."

Mrs. Atkins' smile faded. "I see. Well. Maybe another time."

"Yes. Maybe." Jill yanked Squeak away from Barney and hurried along the sidewalk.

"You were longer than usual," Mrs. Lacey said. She looked closely at Jill. "You look a mite flustered. What's the matter?"

"Nothing. We went to the dime store. And then Squeak wanted to make friends with the dog near the corner. That's why we're late. I'm sorry I worried you."

"Oh, I know Squeak's always in good hands with you. That must've been the Atkinses' dog . . ."

"It was. Mrs. Atkins came out . . . and . . . and . . . her daughter . . ."

"Ah . . . She's a good girl. Helps her ma around the place. Lonely, though. Both of them." She shook her head.

"Does the girl . . . Dede . . . does she have any sisters?"

"No. There's just her and her ma, now."

Jill started down the steps. "Oh, I almost forgot, Mom said she and Dad would like to visit tomorrow night . . ."

"I'll be here!"

Jill walked home slowly, remembering how quiet it'd been when she and Mom had been all alone in the house. It must be pretty boring for that girl Dede. Only, she thought, maybe if you're a retard you don't notice things like that.

"When'll you get to work nearer home?" she asked Dad that evening.

"It won't be long, sweetheart. It's just, when you're new, you're low man on the totem pole. That's why I'm stuck way up in Pawnatucket. But if they see I'm doing really good work, maybe they'll shift me nearer home for the next job." He looked over at Mom. "I don't like being away from home. I miss you. Very much. And it's no fun living in a motel and watching TV reruns night after night." He sighed. "But it's a living. I wouldn't want to be out of work again. Not with a growing family." He didn't say any more for a minute. Then he clapped his hands together. "Now. Who's coming swimming with me tomorrow?"

"Yeah!"

"Joe, we've got to go to the market tomorrow. We're out of everything and with the car gone all week, I can't . . ."

"Honey, there'll be time after the pool, I promise." He looked at her and smiled. "And I haven't forgotten about painting the baby's room, Peg. I know you want to see it ready. I'll start on Sunday. But it'd do us all good to take a break and spend the day together. And I guess the baby's in no hurry — he won't be here till February."

"You're right, Joe," Mom said. "I don't know why I'm so impatient. I want everything perfect right away and I know it's silly . . ."

He stretched out his hand. "Let's you and I go for a stroll now it's cooler. The kids can clean up the kitchen." They walked out together.

Next morning, the heat lay heavily over everything. You could see it, shimmering up off the sidewalk, steaming out of the dewy grass. The leaves of the trees hung down. Nothing moved. Even the birds weren't flying.

Squeak's tongue hung out as he panted up the porch steps after their walk. Jill ran the water till it was very cold and Squeak lapped at it as if he'd never stop.

"I'll be back about five," she called to Mrs. Lacey. "We're going to the pool for the day."

Mrs. Lacey waved limply from the couch.

Mom had packed cold cuts and hard-boiled eggs and lemonade and apples for lunch, so they could stay at the pool. They staked out a spot for themselves on the grass and Mom lay right down and closed her eyes. Dad jumped into the pool with such a splash you'd have thought he'd empty it. The boys went off to look for Ed Kelleher and his friends. Jill slid into the water and floated on her back with her eyes shut against the sun. Cool. Cool. It was good not to be painting . . .

Later, as they sat around eating, Larry said, "Hey, Jill. Ed says he saw you talking to a retard yesterday."

"So?"

"So how come you're so friendly with a retard?"

"I'm not so friendly. I was only there because Squeak and her dog liked each other." Jill stopped peeling her hard-boiled egg.

"She can't find anyone else to be her friend, Lar." Tom grinned.

"She's not my friend, dummy. I told you."

"I'd say it was a perfect match."

"Shut up."

"Cut it out, all of you," Dad interrupted. "This conversation's going nowhere." He glanced at Mom, who had eaten her sandwich and lain back down. "Anyway, I don't want you disturbing your mother." He got up and dove into the pool.

Suddenly, there was loud laughter nearby.

"It's Kelleher," Tom said.

"And Parker and Rusty what's-his-name."

The three boys were throwing a beach ball around in a circle. Dede Atkins was running heavily from one to the other as she tried to catch up with it.

"Come on, old Dede. Try harder!" Ed jeered.

Dan and Rusty were chanting: "Deedee-dum, deedee-dum, deedee-dumb dumb dumb!"

"That's mean," Jill said. "Mom? Tell them."

"I don't want to get into it," Mom said, without opening her eyes. "Where's her mother? She ought to be watching."

"Aw — they're not doing anything bad," Larry said. "She doesn't know the difference anyway."

"How do you know?" Jill felt her face getting hot as she watched Dede stumble around the circle. Just then, Dede tripped and sprawled on the ground.

"That's it!" Jill jumped up and gave Ed Kelleher a push that sent him barreling into Dan.

"Hey!" he yelled.

She snatched up the beach ball and bent over Dede. "It's okay. I've got your ball back. Come on."

Dede got up slowly. There were tears in her eyes. She wiped her nose with the back of her hand. "Hi."

"Show me where your mother is. I'll take you back to her."

"Goody-goody!" Ed shouted.

Jill turned her back on him and walked Dede away.

Dede pointed to a shady spot near the fence and Jill recognized Mrs. Atkins. She was sitting in a beach chair reading a magazine. She looked up when they came near.

"Oh, Dede, there you are. I lost sight of you for a moment or two. I see you've found a friend . . ." She peered at Jill. "You're the girl with the dog."

"Yes, Jill Harvey. Mrs. Atkins, some kids were being mean to Dede. That's why I brought her back to you."

Mrs. Atkins' face tightened. "Are you all right, Dede?" she asked quickly.

"Yeh."

"Thank you, Jill. I . . . I only lost sight of her for a very short while. I wasn't worried because she knows how to swim . . . You'd think these kids could find something better to do. I should have been paying closer attention, but it's hard to watch all the time. I'm very much obliged to you." Her voice was sharp.

Jill talked quickly. "I'm sorry, Mrs. Atkins. They were . . . you know . . . just teasing. They weren't thinking, they didn't mean . . ." I must be crazy, she thought, sticking up for Ed Kelleher and the others. A moment ago she'd been so mad at them. But, in a way, she could see what made them do what they'd done. "Dede's okay now," she told Mrs. Atkins. "I have to go back . . . but I'll try to watch out for her. I'm . . . sorry."

She went back to the others and finished peeling her hard-boiled egg.

Four

Everything was very quiet up and down the street. The paint on Mrs. Lacey's gate had stuck in the heat and Jill had to give it a shove.

Mrs. Lacey was sitting on her couch with her eyes closed.

"Come on, Squeak," Jill whispered. "Time for your walk. Let's go."

They went up the street as usual and back down the other side. They turned at Main and, when they got to Dede's house, Barney was waiting in his yard and he and Squeak greeted each other through the fence pickets. Dede was on her steps, shelling peas into a bowl.

"Want one?" She held out her hand.

"No, thanks."

"Want a cookie?"

"No." Jill pulled Squeak away from the fence. "I have to go."

Mrs. Lacey was still asleep. Jill filled Squeak's bowl as quietly as she could so as not to wake her. Then she tiptoed down the path to the gate and turned to wave. But Squeak hadn't curled up in his basket the way he usually did. He was standing at the top of the steps, whining.

"Ssh! Lie down, Squeak!"

The little dog started down the steps toward her; then he retreated into the porch, whimpering.

"Be quiet!" Jill went back up the steps. Squeak was trembling. His tail was tucked between his legs, dragging his little body down against the ground. "Are you sick?" Jill bent to touch him. "Do you have heat stroke?"

Jill tiptoed along the porch. "Mrs. Lacey," she said softly, "Mrs. Lacey . . ." Mrs. Lacey was fast asleep. "I think Squeak's sick. Could you wake up for a moment . . . Mrs. Lacey?"

Mrs. Lacey stayed the way she was, in the corner of the couch, her hands folded in her lap, her head resting a little sideways on the cushion.

Jill looked at Squeak uneasily. The dog was shivering from one end to the other. "Mrs. Lacey, please wake up." Jill touched her hand. It was cold.

A slow pounding started in Jill's chest. "Mrs. Lacey," she breathed. "Please . . ." She pulled a little at the old woman's sleeve. "Oh . . . please . . ." Nothing. Mrs. Lacey didn't move. Or speak. Or . . . "Oh . . . do-on't . . ." Jill begged. But she knew. She looked at the still face and the quiet figure and she knew. Mrs. Lacey wasn't there any more. "Oh . . ." Squeak had known right away.

Fleeing then. Fleeing down the steps. Away from Mrs. Lacey sitting so quietly. Home . . . Dad would know what to do . . . No. They'd gone to the supermarket. Oo-oh . . . where? Dede. She'd seen Dede. Fleeing back down the block to Dede's. Everything a blur . . . calling it out as she flew up the path. Then running. Mrs. Atkins and Dede and Jill, running back to Mrs. Lacey's so that the quiet, quiet figure shouldn't be left alone.

Mrs. Atkins saw right away how things were and went to the telephone.

Jill stayed close to Mrs. Lacey. She had to keep her company until it was . . . time to go. She shivered next to her on this sticky hot evening. She stared at Mrs. Lacey, as if by doing so she could make an eyelash flicker or a smile spread over that peaceful face. Nothing.

She didn't cry. There was a wall across her throat and the tears dammed up behind it. Little dry gasps came instead, as if she couldn't quite catch her breath. Then she felt the warmth of Dede's body at her side. And Dede's hand on hers, patting her gently over and over.

"It's okay," Dede said. "It's okay. It's okay."

And Jill clutched her hand and held on hard until the ambulance came.

Suddenly Mom and Dad were there.

"Oh, Momma! She's dead, Momma. She was alive this morning and now she's dead . . ." Jill felt Mom's arms go around her. She leaned into her. Across Mom's shoulder she could see Dad shaking hands with Mrs. Atkins. The gesture seemed all out of place.

"Mom . . . the Atkinses are here . . . I thought you weren't home . . . They live near so I went and got them . . ."

"Oh. Oh, honey . . . I'm sorry. But we're here now . . ."

Dad brought the Atkinses over. "Peg, this is Mrs. Atkins. She called us."

Mom shook her hand. "Thank you so much," she said stiffly. "It was very kind . . ."

Dede held out her hand, too, but Mom didn't see. Jill took it.

"Mrs. Lacey told us where her family lives," Dad was saying. "We'll be glad to . . ."

The ambulance men brought up their stretcher and lifted Mrs. Lacey onto it. Gently — as if she could feel what they were doing. Very carefully, they carried Mrs. Lacey to the ambulance, and it took her away.

"That's very good of you," Mrs. Atkins said. "I think I should get Dede home now, if there's nothing you need us for . . ."

"No. Nothing," Mom said. "We can manage. Thank you."

Jill sat on the edge of the couch listening to Mom on the telephone inside, calling Mrs. Lacey's family. It didn't seem right for them to be poking around in Mrs. Lacey's house and looking in her address book. Tremors like little waves breaking on hard sand ran through Jill without stopping. Squeak pressed close against her leg.

After a while, Mom came out. Her face was pale and sharp with strain. "We'll go soon, honey," she said. "Just a couple of people calling back and then we'll go home." She massaged Jill's rigid back. "Oh, honey. Poor baby. I . . . I wish I could . . ." She turned away and went back inside.

Dad appeared in the doorway. He stood there for a moment, then came and lifted Jill off the couch as if she were three instead of eleven. And he sat down and folded her into his lap the way he used to when she was little. He didn't say anything. Just held her.

After a while, he spoke. "Jilly," he said softly, "I want to try to explain . . . It's something I think will help you now . . . There are a lot of things people have to deal with in their lives.

There's a kind of pattern, you know. You see it as you get older. I mean . . . well, all through your life, wherever you are in it, you . . . you're already getting ready for the next stage . . . not even realizing, most of the time." He stroked her shoulder. "You're my Jilly, right? Eleven years old and still my little girl? But, inside, you've begun getting ready to grow into a woman. And then . . . well, how about your mother? All set with our family — and now all of a sudden getting ready to bring a new baby into the world. And that baby! Well, I guess he's got a whole lot of things to get ready for!" He laughed softly. "Me, too!" His voice rumbled against her back.

Jill began to relax against him. The thought of Mrs. Lacey so still, so still . . . the jangling telephone inside the house, the passers-by pausing on the sidewalk — all blurred into the background as her father talked. "That's how it was with Mrs. Lacey, honey. She knew she was going to die. Everyone old knows that . . . knows it's something they must get ready for, just like everything else they've ever done. Of course some are better at it than others. But they all know it's coming. . . The way I see it, Mrs. Lacey had herself all set, except for one thing. Squeak. You see, she had to figure out what was going to happen to Squeak . . ."

Jill's heart jumped against the wall in her

throat. She leaned down and touched Squeak's silky back. He whimpered and snuggled closer.

Dad took her face in his hand and turned it so he could look right into her eyes. "Honey . . . I think Mrs. Lacey had held on for quite a while . . . looking for someone. She must've seen a lot of people come and go past her porch but none of them was quite what she was looking for. Then she spotted you, and I can just imagine her watching you going up and down the street doing errands for Mom . . . And maybe she liked your face. And after she'd talked to you, maybe she liked you more, and she decided to see how Squeak would take to you. Well, you know how well you two hit it off — she could see that right away — and I think she figured she'd found the person who'd look after Squeak for her when she was gone."

"She never said."

"I know, honey. She wouldn't have wanted to scare you. Or make you sad. But I reckon in her heart she knew she could count on you and . . . and . . . once she got the two of you matched up, well, that was the last thing she had left to do. Then she could let go."

They locked up Mrs. Lacey's house and went home in the warm darkness. The boys met them on the porch. "We made supper," Tom said. The first stars were twinkling overhead. Mrs. Lacey had pointed out the constellations a few nights before. Jill looked for them. Then she picked up Squeak and went in.

A long time later, with his live little body warm against her, she finally knew they would not see Mrs. Lacey again, and the tears came at last and soaked her pillow.

Five

Dear Susan,

I hope you know it's YOUR TURN TO WRITE!!! But since you haven't and I have a few more things to tell you I'm writing AGAIN.

You know I told you about Mrs. Lacey. Well, on Saturday when I took Squeak home, she was dead. It was awful, I mean, we didn't say good-bye or anything. And I never told her how much I liked her.

Now I can't.

Mom and Dad said I could keep Squeak and yesterday at the funeral her relatives said it would be okay. He's a neat dog.

We had some people back to the house after the funeral. I know it's terrible to say it, but it was like a party. Dad stayed home from work *and it was the first time we got to meet the neighbors.*

Most of the kids here are still gone on vacation. Marla from next door won't be back till school starts. There was one girl at the funeral — Karen McCluskey — but I didn't talk to her because she got upset and had to go home. The only other kid around is Dede Atkins, only she's retarded.

That's all for now. What are you doing? You'd better write or I'm going to be really mad.

Love,
Jill

Jill sat on the porch steps brushing Squeak. She felt quiet inside. The sad feeling was still there but she was all cried out.

"Hi." Dede and Barney stood at the gate.

"Hi. What're you doing?"

"W-we're taking a walk."

"Yeah? Does your mother know you're out by yourself?"

"Sh-she lets me if Barney's with me."

"Where're you going?"

"F-for a walk."

Squeak's tail was going like sixty. Jill laughed. "Look at him. Do you want to go too, Squeak?"

Squeak yapped, his eyes begging.

"Well — is it okay if we come with you, Dede?"

"Yeh."

"Wait a second." Jill ran inside. "I'm going for a walk with Dede," she called upstairs.

"Who?" Mom answered.

"Dede Atkins."

"Oh, honey, I wish . . ." Her voice sounded funny but Jill didn't feel like stopping to figure it out. "Well . . . okay . . ."

On Monday, Jill and Dede and the dogs headed out on their usual walk. They did it every morning now. Today they were going to the dime store. The dogs sensed they were heading toward Main, with all its fascinating smells, and they pulled the girls along faster and faster as they neared the intersection.

The dime store was around the corner and up the block. Jill had the money for a folder tucked in her pocket. She knew just which one she wanted. It had a shiny laminated cover, with a picture of Yosemite National Park on it. It showed Half Dome and the waterfall and a deer hip-deep in the meadow grass, just the way it'd been when they camped there last year. Susan had been with them.

The dime store was crowded.

"The dogs'll have to stay out here. Can you hold the leashes, Dede? I won't be long."

"Okay."

Jill pushed her way through the people and picked out the folder.

At the checkout, someone said, "Hi. Are you Jill Harvey?" It was Karen McCluskey.

"Yes."

"I saw you at Mrs. Lacey's funeral."

"I saw you, too."

"What're you doing?"

"I just bought a folder for school. How about you?"

"I was looking at the records. I'm saving up for the new Elton John. Hey — want to go to Charlie's and get a cone?"

"Sure!" Finally she'd met someone! "I'll get Squeak."

"You got to keep Mrs. Lacey's dog?"

"Yes. Her family said okay."

"You're so lucky! My sister's allergic. It's a pain. We can't have anything with fur, ever."

Outside, Jill called, "Hi, Squeak!" and the little dog jumped against her, yelping a welcome. Jill pulled the folder out of its bag. "I got it, Dede. See?"

"I like it." Dede stroked the smooth cover.

"We're going up the street to get an ice-cream cone."

"I like ice-cream cones."

"Got any money?"

"No."

Jill dug into her pocket to count what she had left. "Karen — do you have any extra?"

"No."

Jill looked up. Karen's voice was flat. "I'm not paying for her," she said.

"Oh . . . er . . ." Jill shuffled the coins in her hand. "It's okay. I've got enough."

"I'm not going into Charlie's with her," Karen said. She spoke as if Dede wasn't even there. The words hung between them like skywriting in the air.

"Well . . . but . . . she walked here with me . . ." Jill glanced at Dede. She was staring at the ground. Shoot! Jill thought. Dede being along is wrecking everything, but I can't just leave her here on Main. You'd think Karen could see that! Why was she making such a big deal out of it, anyway?

"Well, then . . . I guess we don't have time for a cone right now," Jill said. "Um . . . I forgot I told my mom I'd be right back."

Dede's face clouded. "No ice cream?"

"Maybe tomorrow." She took Squeak's leash from Dede. "Come on, Dede. I'll see you, Karen."

"See you," Karen said.

Jill dropped Dede at her house. Mrs. Atkins looked up from weeding the flower bed. "I just think it's lovely you two girls are getting together all the time."

44

Jill said, "Oh . . . I have to take Squeak out anyway." That sounded mean. She really did enjoy their walks. It was just she always felt she had to be holding Mrs. Atkins off.

On the way home, Jill looked back a couple of times, thinking she might see Karen. But she didn't. Karen was probably sitting in Charlie's right now with another friend. I bet she's got a million, Jill thought. She doesn't need me.

Mom was on the front porch, repairing a chair seat.

"I met Karen McCluskey, Mom."

"Great! Where?"

"In the dime store. She's nice. She came up and talked to me. She wanted to go for a cone."

"Did you have enough money with you?"

"Yes, only I was with Dede and Karen didn't want her along . . ."

"So you didn't go?" Mom looped the rush through the hole in the center of the chair seat and yanked it tight. "You know, Jill, you're really handicapping yourself, spending all your time with that girl." She frowned at the chair, undid what she'd just done and started over.

"It's not *all* my time. Anyway, up till now, I didn't know anyone else. You want a soda?"

"No. I'm watching what I eat. Because of the baby." A shadow passed across her face. "You never know what's in that stuff . . . chemicals, additives, who knows what . . ."

Jill shook her head. "They wouldn't be allowed to sell it if there was anything wrong with it. Think of all the millions and trillions of sodas people drink every day!"

"I'm just being extra careful, that's all."

Jill laughed. "Well, since I'm not having a baby, can I just go ahead? Hey, maybe I'll call Karen — see if she's home yet."

"You do that. I'd like to see somebody . . . else around here once in a while."

Jill looked up Karen's number and dialed. Karen answered.

"Karen? It's Jill."

"Oh. Hi."

"I just wanted to say . . . well, it was too bad . . . about just now, I mean. The thing is, I couldn't dump Dede. She's not used to being on Main."

"Oh. Well, the thing is, that kid gives me the creeps — the way she looks and the way she talks. I mean, when you're with her, doesn't everyone stare all the time?"

"Maybe they do, a little. I guess I've gotten used to being with her and I don't notice. Anyway. You want to do something after lunch?"

"Sure. How about the pool?"

"Great. We can ride our bikes."

"Okay. I'll see you about two at your house. Bye."

Jill hung up and hugged Squeak.

Six

"Why don't you wear that nice green skirt and a white blouse?"

"Mo-om. No one wears skirts to school!"

"I just think it's silly to wear long pants on a hot September day."

"Well, I'm going to."

Mom headed for the door. "I give up!"

Jill had laid everything out on the bed ready for the morning. Blue jeans, soft and faded just right. A blue plaid shirt which matched. Sneakers freshly washed and smelling good. Folder. Pencils. Assignment notebook. She was ready.

She and Mom had been to the York Falls Elementary School two weeks before to register for sixth grade. It was at the top of a hilly street

— a square, yellow-brick building with an asphalt playground. There were a few faded hopscotch squares, a couple of seesaws and a set of swings for the little kids, some rusty basketball hoops with no nets for the rest.

"Doesn't look too bad," Mom said.

Jill didn't say a word. It looked horrible. And there was something else. In California, the elementary and middle schools had been on the same grounds. Tom and Larry had been somewhere near. But here the junior high was across town. It gave her a lonesome feeling, thinking about it . . .

The telephone rang. Too early to be Dad calling from Pawnatucket.

"Ji-ill. It's for you."

"Who is it?"

"Karen, I think."

"Hello?"

"Hi. It's Karen."

"Oh! Hi!"

"Do you want some company walking to school tomorrow?"

"Sure. Thanks."

"What're you wearing?"

"Jeans. And a blue plaid shirt."

"I won't wear blue, then."

"Okay."

"I have to go now. Have to go get my little sister new shoes. What fun!"

48

"Will you pick me up? What time?"

"Oh, yeah. I forgot. About eight-thirty. See you."

"See you."

Jill found Mom in the kitchen. "Karen's picking me up in the morning."

"That's good. She seems like a really nice girl. I'm glad you've made friends with her." She laughed. "I'd begun to think you'd never spend your time with anyone but Dede . . ."

Jill went back upstairs. Tom was getting his school stuff together. He zipped a couple of pens and a pencil inside his blue folder.

"Got everything?" Jill asked.

"Guess so," Tom said. "I'll find out soon enough." He grinned. "How about you? It's going to feel pretty funny, being in a new school, huh?"

"I guess so." Jill fidgeted in the doorway. "Tom . . . have you noticed the way Mom acts around Dede?"

"What way?"

"Well, she acts weird. Stiff, kind of."

"Yeah?"

"And she's always harping at me about getting some other friends. And I'm going to . . . I mean, it's not like Dede's the only kid I'll know around here . . . I already know Karen. But Mom seems to have some kind of hangup about Dede."

49

"I hadn't noticed. I don't know . . . maybe she thinks you'll start acting like her."

"Well, that'd be pretty dumb! But I don't think that's it. No . . . it's almost as if she was . . . scared of her. You'd think she could see there's nothing scary about Dede."

"Maybe your're imagining it. If you want to know, I don't get why you hang around with Dede myself."

Jill wiggled herself into his beanbag chair. "Well, now I'm used to the way she is, she's sort of . . . comfortable to be with. She's quiet. She never wants anything. And she's never mean. I never heard her say one mean thing about anybody. And . . . well, I know it sounds funny . . . but she listens when I talk. But supposing I don't want to talk, say, just walk along . . . that's okay with her, too."

"I see what you mean," Tom said. "Well, maybe it's just a question of Mom getting used to her, too."

"She never will, the way she's going," Jill said.

At eight-thirty the next morning, Karen rang the doorbell. She was wearing a red bandana-print shirt.

"Hi, Karen!" Mom had combed her hair out as if this were some big social occasion. And she kept smiling. "How nice of you to take Jill along with you. How thoughtful!"

Karen looked embarrassed.

"We have to go, Mom," Jill said quickly. "Don't forget to walk Squeak."

"I won't. I need the exercise as much as he does. Have a good day!" Mom was being pretty charming, considering how she usually acted in the morning. Though, as Jill thought about it, Mom was looking better at breakfast time lately. The baby must be settling down.

When they got outside, Karen said, "We'd better stop for Marla."

"She's back?"

"Yes. She called last night to be sure we walked to school together."

"What's she like? Her mother's sort of glamorous — like some movie star or something."

"Yeah. Well . . . Marla's pretty, I guess. She has naturally curly hair . . . My mother says her mother used to be a dancer. Laraine Marshall, that's her stage name. Marla calls her Laraine, if you can believe it! And her grandma, the one in Boston, was a Rockette at Radio City Music Hall, and pretty famous, Marla says."

"They sure don't sound like the York Falls type!" Jill laughed.

"They came to York Falls after Mrs. Burns got married to Mr. Burns, and then Marla and her mom just stayed on after the split."

"Did you ever see him?"

"No. He went away ages ago. My mother says he was nice. But he decided to live in Nebraska — he sells fertilizer — and Mrs. Burns wouldn't go because of her career. Only as far as I can see she doesn't have one!"

"She didn't go back to being a dancer?"

"No. Maybe it was hard to do, with a kid. I think she works sometimes."

They climbed Marla's steps. The door flew open and Marla ran out and hugged Karen.

"Oh, Karen, I missed you absolutely dreadfully!" she cried. "Of course it was fabulous in Boston. But it's even more fabulous to be back with my friends!"

Nobody talks that way, Jill thought. She's not for real. She stared, fascinated. Marla was small and pretty. Short blond curly hair. Big blue eyes. She chattered on at Karen, holding on tight. It's . . . it's like she rehearsed it, Jill decided. Karen rolled her eyes and waited for Marla to let go.

She did finally and turned to Jill. Jill backed up a couple of steps.

"And you're Jill," Marla said in a whispery voice. "Laraine told me she'd met you. And she's seen your cute brothers in the yard. I think it's just great you're next door. Much more fun than that old drag, Mrs. Miller." She made a face. Then looking straight into Jill's eyes, she said, "I guess you and Karen have been doing just everything together while I've been away." Funny the way she said it, almost threatening.

"Oh, no," Karen said quickly. "We only met a few days ago."

Mrs. Burns appeared in the doorway. She leaned against it, her pink chiffon robe floating around her. She waved a glass of orange juice at the girls. "Bye, sweets," she said huskily to Marla. "Don't be late home. Al is taking us out to dinner."

Marla didn't answer. She went down the steps without looking back. Karen and Jill hurried to catch up. She was looking mad.

"What's the matter, Marla?" Karen asked.

"She always makes him take me. And I know he doesn't want me along. Why would he? I have to sit there and watch him making eyes at her all through dinner. I hate it!" She marched along.

Jill glanced at Karen, who shrugged. Better change the subject, Jill thought. She said, "That's a neat skirt, Marla." It was made of white pleated nylon and Marla had a navy and white polka-dotted blouse to match.

Marla slowed down. "Do you like it? My grandma got it for me. She likes skirts on me. She says I have to show my legs to advantage if I'm going to be a dancer."

"Are you?"

"I guess so. Our whole family dances."

"She takes tap and ballet and modern and lots of other stuff, too," Karen said.

"My grandma says she's going to see me center stage one day," Marla said. "She says that's all she's living for, to see me center stage, the way she used to be . . ."

A school bus passed them. The kids inside were knocking on the windows.

"It's the retards' bus," Karen said. "Going to Pearson."

Each window framed a face. Some were grinning. Some were ugly. Some were . . . empty. Dede was waving in the back window. Jill waved back.

"Ugh!" Marla said. "How can you wave at them? I can't even look at them, they're so gross."

Dede didn't look so gross to Jill any more.

"They can't help the way they look," she said.

Seven

Tom put down his paint brush. "When can we go to Boston, Dad?"

"Why do you want to go to Boston?"

Jill had to smile. When Dad didn't want to answer a question he always replied with another. And before you knew it, the conversation had gone off in a different direction.

"Well, I'd just like to see it, that's all," Tom said. "I mean, it's old and it's big and . . . and anyway, I'd just like to see some place different from York Falls! We moved here three months ago and we haven't been any place!"

"Let's do it, Dad," Larry said. "We could leave real early and we'd be there in . . . How far is it from here?"

"Oh — I'd say about eighty miles."

"We could be there in a couple of hours. Even less. And we could walk all over and go to a Boston College game . . ."

"And how do you think your mother would handle all that in her condition? No. We'll have to wait till the spring. Anyway, there's plenty to keep us busy right here for a while." Dad turned back to the molding near the ceiling and dabbed carefully at it with a fresh brushful of paint.

Jill sighed. She wanted to go to Boston, too. It was dumb living so near a famous place without having gone there. Marla was always talking about Boston.

Very slowly, Jill worked her brush down a strut between the windowpanes. She didn't want one drop of the paint beading onto the glass.

"Can I go when I finish this radiator, Dad?" Larry asked. "Everybody's down at Dan's."

"We'll see," Dad said, from his ladder. "There's still a lot to do. I want this baby's room finished today."

"Other kids don't have to work so much on Saturdays," Tom grumbled. "You're gone all week with the car and then every weekend when we could go somewhere like Boston you bring home a big list of jobs for us to do instead."

Jill waited for Dad to get mad. He frowned. But all he said was, "It's good experience for you, Tom."

She stood back to look at her work. No smudges, no spots. The October sun warmed her through the glass. Marla was out in her back-yard, watching Leroi, her poodle, smooshing through the fallen leaves. Boy, she thought, if that was me I'd jump right into those leaves and fall down so they covered me up and no one would even know I was there. I wouldn't just stand around letting Leroi have all the fun. But she knew why Marla wasn't jumping in the leaves. She was dressed in her red skirt with the anchor on it and a blue blazer with a gold crest on the pocket. She'd be leaving for her ballet lesson at eleven. After that, she had to go to her creative drama session. Later in the afternoon, she had a piano lesson.

"I'm being groomed," she'd told Jill. "I need to know all these things if I'm going on the stage." Being groomed didn't seem like much fun. It used up every Saturday.

Jill knocked on the window. Marla looked up and waved.

"Wait," Jill mouthed through the glass. She ran down the stairs and out into the yard. "Marla! Hey, Marla?"

Marla came over to the fence. "What?"

"Do you know yet if you can come to my slumber party Friday?"

"I asked Laraine, but I didn't really get an answer yet."

"What do you mean?"

"Well . . ." Marla looked embarrassed. "She wouldn't say yes and she wouldn't say no. But I do want to come, Jill."

"It's going to be fun. Just you and Karen and Connie and me. And we'll have pizza and popcorn and listen to records. It's what I asked for instead of a birthday party. I'm too old for birthday parties."

"I'll ask again. I should've known not to ask her in the evening. She's always . . . tired in the evening. I'll let you know today for sure."

"Okay, I have to get back to painting. We're finishing the baby's room."

"That's so neat — your mother having a baby — you're lucky! Isn't your mother absolutely thrilled?" Marla's eyes shone.

"I guess so. She doesn't talk about it much."

"I think it's fabulous! What do you hope it'll be?"

Jill smiled. "Just a baby. I don't really care if it's a boy or a girl. Oh — I guess I'd rather have a baby sister . . ."

"That's what I'd want. I've always wanted a sister . . . only there's no way I'm going to get one unless my mother marries again . . ."

"Marla! Marla, did you tie Leroi up?" Mrs. Burns beckoned from the door. "Let's go! Grandma wouldn't like you to be late for your lessons."

"Oh . . . okay," Marla called. "I'll let you know about the party," she told Jill.

"It's beautiful," Mom said from the doorway.

"And it's finished," said Dad. "Except for that radiator. I'll do that one." They all stood admiring the sunny yellow walls and white trim. "Okay, boys, wash your brushes and take the afternoon off."

Jill said, "I'm going to rake up leaves and make big jumping piles."

"Fine, honey," Mom said. "But take Squeak for a walk, first, will you? He hasn't been out today."

"Okay. We'll go down to Charlie's for a cone."

Charlie's was crowded, but the only people Jill knew were Mrs. Atkins and Dede, who were having a milkshake at the counter.

"Jill! How are you?" Mrs. Atkins said. "We haven't seen much of you since school started."

Jill was embarrassed because it was true. "I know," she said. "I've been pretty busy . . ." There was homework. And watching TV at Karen's. And working out on Marla's trampoline . . . Mrs. Atkins kept smiling. "Uh . . . want to walk back to my house now, Dede? I was planning to make some leaf piles and jump in them."

"Yeh." Dede beamed. "Let's make some leaf piles and j-jump in them."

"Okay, Mrs. Atkins?"

"It's a lovely idea, Jill. A lovely idea!" Jill thought, she doesn't have to pat my shoulder like that.

At Dede's house, they called Barney and then walked up Maple together, the way they used to, Barney and Squeak leading the way.

"I'll find the rakes," Jill said. "You let the dogs loose out back."

They piled the leaves high and Jill took the first jump, swooping stomach first. Leaves flew around her, then showered down like golden rain from the blue sky. Barney plunged in after her and licked her face anxiously, while Squeak yapped from the edge.

"Yuck, Barney!" Jill pushed him off and he bounded away. She lay on her back in the leaves and stared at a bird planing slowly above her. "This is great. I could stay here for a hundred years . . . a hundred years . . ."

"Yeh." Dede leaned on her rake. Her face was red from her hard work and her nose was running. She never noticed when her nose ran.

"You know, I didn't think I'd like it here, Dede. I thought I'd always want to go back to California." She laughed. "Do you know, I just thought of something. My friend Susan never wrote to me once and I was really mad . . . I mean, she'd been my best friend . . . but just now I realized I haven't thought of her for weeks!"

"Yeh?"

"Yeah. And do you know something else? I'm even beginning to like this dumb town. I mean, school's not bad . . . I know most of the stuff . . . and I'm in the power group in spelling."

"Th-that's good."

"Jump into the leaves, Dede. It's fun."

Dede put down her rake, took a run and landed heavily beside Jill. She sneezed as the leaves fountained up around her. Jill fished in her pocket for a tissue.

"Here. Blow your nose. I get to sit next to Connie Ward in science. She's my lab partner. Marla's partner is Tommy Williamson — of course she gets a boy! I wish Karen was in our room so we were all together. I wish we had her instead of that creepy Mary Poletti who always copies over my shoulder. Karen's in our gym class, though . . ."

Dede listened to her and smiled up at the sky, wheezing a little from the dust in the leaves. Jill thought of the things they did in gym. Dede wouldn't be any good at gym. Too fat. She'd get out of breath right away.

"Do you ever have gym, Dede?"

"Yeh."

"Like — what do you do?"

"W-we run . . . and walk backward. Sometimes we j-jump." Dede's face was serious. "W-we're training."

"Training? What for?"

"Special Olympics."

"Olympics! That's crazy. How could you guys be in the Olympics?"

Dede shook her head in puzzlement. "I don't know."

Jill thought, she gets some pretty weird ideas into her head sometimes. "Tell me some more, Dede," she said. "What do you do when you're not in gym? Do you do arithmetic? Stuff like that?"

"Yeh." Dede smiled. "I know my numbers up to ten. I can wr-write them. And I can write Dede. D-E-D-E."

"That's *good!* You'll have to show me."

"Yeh."

"Anything else?"

Dede frowned, thinking. "We play store. And we c-cook." She sat up. "And we g-grow things."

"What? Vegetables, flowers?"

"Yeh. I like that best. I l-love flowers." Dede smiled. "They're j-just seeds in the beginning. I water them and I water them and then th-they grow into fl-flowers for me."

It was the longest sentence Jill had ever heard her say. Dede shut her eyes and lay back in the leaves. Jill did too.

The sun filtered down through the trees. It felt good on her closed eyelids. She listened. Mr. Garland was clipping his hedge. Somewhere a cat was meowing. Larry's radio was tuned to the B.C. game. Leroi was barking over in Marla's yard. Jill rolled over and the leaves crackled around her.

"Let's try and fool old Barney, Dede. I'll cover you up and we'll see if he thinks you've gone home without him."

"Okay."

Jill hollowed out a place in the leaf pile and Dede got into it. "Keep still now," Jill said, as she raked the leaves, "or Barney will figure it out."

Soon she couldn't see Dede at all.

"Hey, Barney!" Jill called. "Where's Dede? Where's she gone?"

Barney wagged his tail. "I don't think we've fooled him," Jill said out of the side of her mouth. The leaf pile stirred a little. Barney's tail wagged harder. He started sniffing around the edge of the leaves, playing the game.

"Jill! Hey, Jill!" Marla waved over the fence.

"Hi. You're home early."

"I know. I forgot my piano music. Laraine's so mad!"

"Can you come over?"

"Yes. Only I still have to have my piano lesson. I thought I'd get out of it. But I wanted to tell you . . . I asked her and I can. Come to your party, I mean. Well, I'd better go. I'll come over as soon as I get. . ."

The leaves exploded as Barney plunged into the middle of the pile, his tail swishing them in all directions. Dede popped up like a jack-in-the-box. Marla's smile froze on her face.

"We'll see you when you get back," Jill called.

Marla said stiffly, "I didn't know . . . I mean . . . I forgot — I have to do something important . . ." She stared at Dede and said loudly, "Anyway. All I wanted to do was tell you I can come to your party." She turned and walked into her house.

"Party?" Dede said.

Why'd she have to say that? She knows I haven't asked Dede, Jill thought. "Dede! Your hair is all full of leaves and twigs and junk," she said.

"What party?" Dede asked.

Marla's so mean, Jill thought angrily. "Oh . . . it's not a party really . . . just a . . . sleepover . . . you know . . ."

"Can I come?"

"Well, the thing is, Dede . . . well, I can only have just a couple of kids and . . . well, you can't . . . this time, I mean. . ."

"I never w-went to a party," Dede said, pulling leaves out of her hair.

"Never?"

"N-nobody asked me."

"Oh." Jill felt rotten. She tried picturing Dede at her slumber party. No. She'd be so out of it, it wasn't funny.

"Let's go inside and see what there is to eat," Jill said.

"Yeh! I'm h-hungry!"

Mom was peeling potatoes in the kitchen.

"What's to eat, Mom?"

"You'd better think about your weight, Jill. You're always eating these days." She turned. "Oh. Dede, uh . . . hello." She put down the half-peeled potato, wiped her hands dry and headed for the door. "Make yourselves a sandwich," she said. "I'll get out of your way. I'll be upstairs . . ."

"Hi," Dede said to Mom's back.

"Here, Dede," Jill said, handing her a can from the refrigerator. They made tunafish sandwiches and Jill poured some apple juice. "Let's go back outside," she said. Mo-om, it's safe to come down now, she thought.

The girls sat in the sunshine with the dogs stretched out beside them.

"I l-like tuna," Dede said, taking a bite out of her sandwich.

"Yes, it's good. And I like steak . . ."

"Yeh."

". . . and French fries . . . and cheese-cake . . ."

"Yeh . . . and-and b-brownies . . ." Dede grinned, taking another bite. As she did, a blur of white shot between them. The sandwich vanished from her hand.

Jill jumped up. "Leroi! Bad dog! How did you get over here?" Barney and Squeak barked furiously at Leroi, but he just stood there, licking his lips. "I don't believe it! He's grinning at us! You're a thief, Leroi! Bad dog!" Jill turned to Dede. "He must've dug a hole under the fence. I'd better. . . ." She stared. Dede's face was scrunched up. She was rocking. Backward and forward. Backward and forward. "What're you doing?"

"*Ah . . . ah . . . ah . . .*"

"What is it? Leroi didn't hurt you, did he? Let me look."

Dede's hand was held tightly against her body as she hugged herself and rocked and rocked. Jill peeled it away. One of the fingers was a bit red.

"Bad Leroi! Bad dog!" Jill rubbed Dede's finger gently. "It's just grazed a little. It's not bleeding. Look . . . Dede . . ."

Dede wouldn't look. "*Ah . . . ah . . . ah . . .*"

"He didn't mean it. He's really a nice dog. I guess he just saw that sandwich and he wanted it. . . Maybe Marla forgot to feed him or something. . ." Jill talked fast. She had to make Dede forget her finger — think about something else. "Dede, stop crying. I guess I'd better take him back. Dede . . . hey, do you want to put a band-aid on it? Come on . . . we'll take Leroi home and tie him up and . . . Dede . . ."

"*Ah . . . ah . . .*" Dede was going on and on as if she'd cry forever. Jill ran inside the house.

"Mom!" she called up the stairs. "Leroi snapped at Dede's finger and she's crying and I can't make her stop. Can you come out?"

"Oh, honey . . . I just lay down . . . Can't you try . . . ?"

"No. I've been trying."

"Daddy'll come. I'm undressed . . . Get her a band-aid. They're in the bathroom cabinet."

"I *am* getting her a band-aid. But I guess she really got scared or something. . ."

"Daddy's coming."

Dad came, wiping his hands on a rag. "What's going on?" He frowned. "What's the matter?"

Jill pointed at Dede, rocking in the grass. He stopped looking mad and ran outside. "Poor kid," he said, hugging Dede.

"*Ah . . . ah . . .*"

He pulled her up gently. "We're going to put something on it, honey."

"*Ah . . . ah . . .*"

Jill put her hands over her ears. She couldn't

67

stand it. "Hey, Dede. Shall I make you another sandwich?"

Dede shook her head. Tears were pouring down her face. It's so weird, Jill thought, she didn't cry this way when the boys were being mean to her . . . I guess she's more used to that. . .

"Do you want me to call your mother?"

Another shake. "*Ah . . . ah . . .*"

"Dede . . . hey, listen! You know what? I'm going to tell you something I was keeping for a surprise . . ."

"*Ah . . . ah . . .*"

"Listen! How can you hear me if you keep crying! You know what's coming to you in the mail pretty soon?"

"*Ah . . .*"

"An invitation to my birthday party in a couple of weeks!"

Dede looked at her. "*. . . Ah . . . a . . .* p-party? M- me?"

"Yes. You!"

"A p-party?"

"I mean it!"

Okay, Jill thought, great! What do I do now? I'm not even having a birthday party in a couple of weeks!

Eight

Jill walked Dede home.

"Mama!" Dede called before they'd even opened the gate. "Mama!"

Mrs. Atkins ran outside, looking worried. "What's the matter?"

"I'm going to a p-party!"

"Party?"

"J-Jill's having a party. She asked me."

Mrs. Atkins looked at Jill. Jill nodded. "You did? How wonderful!"

Jill was embarrassed. "Oh, it's just a little . . ."

Dede said, "It's a b-birthday party!"

"Oh, Jill!" Mrs. Atkins took her hand. "That's lovely of you. Dede'll be so excited. When is it?"

"Er . . . in a couple of weeks. Dede'll be getting an invitation in the mail." Jill wanted to get off the subject, so she told Mrs. Atkins about Leroi. Dede's finger wasn't even red any more. Why didn't I keep my stupid mouth shut, she thought.

She walked slowly home, trying to figure out what she was going to do. The leaves drifted through the hazy afternoon sunlight. It was quiet on Maple — just the whirr of Mr. Garland's lawnmower and the buzz of a cruising airplane.

She let herself in the gate and was halfway up the steps before she heard them.

"I don't understand you at all, Peg. At least you should explain to the kid why you're acting this way. You're confusing her. She can't figure you out and neither can I!" Dad's voice came clearly from the upstairs window.

"I can't . . . I know I'm being silly, Joe. But I don't even want to put it into words . . ."

"Well, it's not fair to her. She's old enough. Why not tell her?"

"I don't want to talk about it — it might bring bad luck!"

"That's plain stupid, Peg. You should know better!" Dad's feet drummed down the stairs and out on to the porch. "Oh." He stopped short. "Jilly. Did . . . ? Yes, you did."

Jill wished he hadn't found her there. It

looked like she was eavesdropping and she wasn't.

"Dad . . . I just got . . ." But she knew her face was giving her away. She'd heard enough to know they'd been fighting about her.

"Okay. This settles it. Come inside, Jilly." Dad put his arm around her shoulders. "Mom's going to have to face up to a few things."

Mom came down the stairs in her bathrobe. She was beginning to lean a little backward to adjust for the extra weight in front. She'd heard. You could tell. "I'm sorry, honey," she said. Jill didn't know if she meant her or Dad. She had a sort of wary look, as if she expected to be hurt.

"Now we're going to sit down and talk this whole thing out," Dad said. What whole thing? "Where are the boys?"

"At Dan's." Mom's face was white.

"Oh. Well . . . This concerns Jill more than them, anyway, because of Dede."

"Joe, I can't."

"Then I will. Sit down, Peg."

Jill sat on the edge of a chair. Something important was happening. She watched them carefully.

"You've been puzzled by your mom's behavior toward Dede, haven't you, Jill?"

Mom had shrunk back into her chair. Like a child in trouble, Jill thought. "It's okay, Dad," she said.

"No. It's not okay. I want this out in the open, where it always should have been. I'm going to tell you what's bothering your mother. You've a right to know. Dede's our neighbor and your friend and she's going to be around. We've got to stop avoiding this issue." He frowned at Mom. She looked away. He spoke quickly. "There was another baby once, Jilly — a long time ago when you were still a baby yourself. Even the boys don't remember. Well . . . maybe Tom . . ." Mom was staring down at her hands, clenched together in her lap. "Anyway, the baby was a girl — your sister — but, when she came . . . well, you could see something had gone wrong somewhere along the way . . ." His voice shook. "It wasn't fair . . . such a little thing . . . she didn't live . . ." He cleared his throat. "Just as well. She'd have had no kind of life . . ." He broke off. He got up and walked abruptly to the window and stared out.

Jill sat very still. She felt oddly relieved. It was as if at last she was hearing something that had been there unspoken from the beginning. She looked at her parents. Mom pinned down in her chair like a butterfly on a board. Dad with his back turned. The silence was smothering. She had to say something.

"I guess Dede reminds you, Mom . . ."

Mom shook her head. "It isn't that, Jilly.

It's . . . it's because of the new baby coming. I'm older this time and that makes it risky. I'm . . . really spooked about it, I guess. So scared the same thing will happen . . . again . . ."

"Was . . . was that baby retarded, like Dede? Is that why you don't want to have her around?"

"No. Not like Dede . . ." She stared at Dad's back. "It's so silly, really . . ."

Jill said, "I don't get it, then. What happened? Do you know what happened?"

"No." Mom's voice was cool as stone.

Dad turned at the sound of it and his face softened. He sat on the arm of Mom's chair and held her. "We don't know," he said. "She . . . her body wasn't properly formed . . ."

"I don't get what Dede has to do with it. I don't understand . . ."

"She would have been retarded. Only it would've been different. And much worse. Blind . . . deaf. Dede's retardation is due to what's called Down's syndrome, which is caused by a set of extra chromosomes in the cells of her body. With our baby, we could only guess at the cause — the doctors said it might have been a virus your mother had . . ."

"Oh. You think maybe our baby will catch what Dede's got?"

"No, no, honey. You can't catch Down's syndrome. What our baby's trouble was, was different. And it might have been caused by a virus Mom had while she was pregnant . . . nothing to do with Dede's type of retardation."

"But you haven't been sick!" Jill burst out. "It would never happen twice. God wouldn't let it happen twice. Whatever it was, that was ten whole years ago — why don't you ask the doctor? Maybe he can find out ahead of time and then you'll know."

"I don't want to know!" Mom's voice was shrill.

"Oh, Mom. Oh, Mom." Jill knelt beside her and held on tight, and realized it was more of a stretch than it used to be. That baby really was there. Out of sight inside, growing in the warm dark. "It'll be all right. I know it, Mom. Everything's different now from then. You're in a new place. You and Dad are even different people from the way you were ten years ago. And I'm big now. I can do a lot of things and we'll all help so you don't get tired. And I'm going to keep Dede out of here, so you won't have to see her."

"Oh, honey, there's no need for that now . . ." Mom gestured helplessly. "You see, all these years I've tried to forget what happened. It was too sad to think about. And I'd just about done it. Even when the new baby started, I could blot out what had happened the last time. But, seeing Dede all the time, well . . . it was like a little voice nagging at me, saying, 'You see what can happen, you see what can happen.' I began looking on her as some kind of jinx." She laughed and the tears brimming in her eyes spilled onto her cheeks. "Your father's right. I was being superstitious. Seeing Dede's not going to affect the way things turn out." She smiled at Dad and Jill felt herself relax.

"The boys should know, too," Mom said quietly. "Now we must tell them."

Nine

"No way!" Karen said, plumping her pillow. "She gives me the creeps!"

Marla got up and lurched around the room, flapping the arms of her pajamas. It was a pretty good imitation of Dede. They all yelled with laughter.

"You're too much, Marla!" Connie screamed.

Marla bowed and climbed back into her sleeping bag.

"Come on, you guys. Quit fooling around. You've got to help me out. I've invited her to a nonexistent party," Jill said.

"Forget about it. She won't remember."

"Yes, she will. She's talked about it every day since, and her mother told Mom how wonderful it was of me to ask her. So I've got to come through."

"Well, count me out!" Karen said, still grinning.

"Come on, Kar. What're you afraid of?"

Karen's grin faded. "I don't know. But I am. I'm not kidding. She *does* give me the creeps. Maybe it's because I don't know what she's going to do. I mean, it's not like with a normal kid who acts the same way you do. Then you can kind of look ahead and . . . be ready. I mean, you know they think the same way you do. Like, supposing I say to you, 'Are you going to watch the soccer game after school?' I know you're either going to say 'Yes, I want to,' or 'No, I have too much homework,' or anyway something that makes sense to me. But if I ask Dede that, she'll say 'Yeh' and all the time not even know what soccer is. Her saying 'Yeh' wouldn't mean anything. How can you talk to a person like that? I don't have any idea what she knows and what she's thinking . . . if she's thinking anything. She lives in a different world from us . . . you know what I mean?"

"I know. But she has feelings, that's for sure. Even if she doesn't understand everything, she knows when someone's unhappy. And she knows when someone's being mean to her. She can get scared, too, just like us. She's sort of the same, only different. I mean, a lot of stuff goes right over her head. But then something that wouldn't bother one of us really gets to her. Like . . . well, the way I got this party idea was because she got scared when Leroi grabbed her sandwich. He didn't really hurt her, but she started crying and she couldn't stop. I tried everything to make her stop and that's when I ended up telling her she was being invited to a party. And that worked. Do you guys realize she's never been asked to a party in her whole life? That's why she's so excited about it . . . There's no reason to be scared of her, Kar. I'm not scared of her and I see her every day."

"I know and I don't get it. I'd be so bored!"

"Well — it's not like it's for hours and hours. I like company when I take Squeak out. And she has to walk Barney. So it just . . . works for both of us. And she's nice. I mean, I never heard her say anything mean. And she gets fun out of little things."

"I don't see how you can stand being seen with her," Marla said. "You know, those slanty eyes and the way she walks . . ."

"Well, it's not catching, for heaven's sakes."

"And the way she talks!" Marla went on. "I can't understand her half the time!"

"Well, you don't listen half the time!"

"What do you talk about?" Connie asked quickly.

"Oh . . . school . . . and people . . . the dogs . . ."

"Duh-duh. Duh-duh . . ." Marla pulled down the corners of her mouth.

"She doesn't talk like that," Jill said. "You're so dumb, Marla. What it comes down to is — are you supposed to be my friends or aren't you?" Jill glared at all of them. "Mom says we can have the party in a couple of weeks. You're already having the sleepover. So, are you going to come or not? I figure I'll ask all the girls in 6B."

"Well," Karen said slowly, "maybe. If everyone else says yes."

"I'll come," Connie said.

"Okay." Marla had stopped making faces. "Okay. I'll come, too. Only because it's you, Jill Harvey. And you owe me!"

Jill wrote out her invitations. She printed Dede's in big letters and drew a bunch of balloons with happy faces, so Dede would know right away that it was the party invitation.

"I hope it goes all right," she said to Mom. "What if the other kids are mean to Dede?"

"We'll tell them to cut it out!" Mom said. "But I think it'd be a good idea to warn the others what to expect."

Twelve girls accepted their invitations and

Jill explained that there'd be someone retarded at the party.

"Retarded? But I've never . . . How? I don't think . . . I couldn't . . ." they said.

"Don't get uptight," Jill said. "She's nice and she's friendly and it's just she's sort of slow picking things up. It'll be okay. I'm figuring out some games that won't be too hard for her. Some of them will seem stupid for kids like us, but if we all go along, it'll be fun. How about it?"

Two of the girls suddenly remembered something else they had to do on that day, but the rest said it was okay with them.

On the day, Dede and Barney were the first to get there. Mom's face froze, just for a moment, when she came out of the house and saw them. She seemed to shiver a little, as if shaking off a spell. Then she hugged Dede around the shoulders, saying, "Good to see you!" Jill let her breath go.

Jill had told Tom and Larry to get lost, but of course they didn't. They hung out the bedroom window and made dumb remarks as the kids arrived. "Aren't you guys supposed to be someplace else?" Jill called up to them. They grinned. "Nope," they said.

She turned back to her friends in the yard. There was something wrong already. Karen and

Connie and Marla, Monica, Frannie, Lisa and Helen, Margaret, Carol and Jackie were standing all together. Dede was standing by herself. She was smiling at them. But they weren't smiling back. They were just staring at her. Frannie whispered behind her hand into Lisa's ear. Lisa snickered.

Jill said quickly, "Hey, let's go out back. Dad's hidden peanuts all over. Whoever finds the most gets a prize."

"I like peanuts," Dede said.

"I like peanuts," Marla mimicked.

"Shut up, Marla." Jill glared at her.

"Okay, you guys," Marla said, with a look. "Remember peanut hunts?"

The others giggled.

Dad distributed paper bags and they spread out.

"I call, the toolshed's mine," Helen said.

"No fair!" Jackie shouted.

"Everyone can look everywhere," Dad said.

"Any up in the tree?" Carol asked.

"Nothing is higher than you can reach from the ground," Jill answered.

They hunted for five minutes, then Dad blew a whistle. "Time to count them up!" Everyone spilled her peanuts out on the grass. Each pile was different. Dede's was nothing but shells. Monica and Jackie snorted.

"That's okay, Dede," Dad said. "I should've

told you not to eat them until after I'd counted them."

"I like peanuts!" Dede said with a big smile.

"Well, I guess you do!" Dad smiled back. Good old Dad! He walked around, counting. "Boy, I feel I'm right back on the job!" he joked. "Looks to me as if Helen's found the most, so she gets the prize." He pulled a little box with a ring in it out of his pocket. Jill had found some good prizes at the thrift shop. "There you go, Helen. But I've got to hand it to Dede. She's way ahead of the rest of you in the eating department!"

Dede beamed.

Dad pulled four sacks of old clothes out on the grass. "Okay," he said. "Next is a relay race. Everyone has to change clothes at each end of the run."

"Dad." Jill pulled at his arm. "I just thought — Dede can't do buttons."

"Oh-oh. . . um . . . okay. I need a judge for this race. Dede — how about it? Will you be the judge?"

"Yeh!"

Dad showed her where to stand.

She's having a good time, Jill thought. It's going to be all right.

Dad blew his whistle and everyone shrieked and giggled and clutched. They fell down and got up and struggled forward. As the last two raced for the finish line, they were very close. Monica made it just ahead of Margaret.

Dede pointed to Monica. "She won!"

"She did not!" Margaret cried. "It was a tie!"

"She won," Dede insisted. "I kn-know."

"What do you know? You don't know anything!" Margaret yelled. "How would a dummy like you know anything!"

"Hey, hey! That's enough of that kind of talk!" Dad spoke quietly, but Margaret shut up, her face red. "Dede is right. Monica's team won."

"You did good, Dede," Jill said in her ear. "Margaret's just acting stupid."

"Yeah."

"Now, we're going to play Duck, Duck, Goose," Dad said.

"Duck, Duck, Go-ose! That's for *first* graders!" Frannie groaned. "I'm not playing."

"Me neither," Lisa said. She always did whatever Frannie did.

Dad said, "Too bad! You two will miss the fun." He didn't try to persuade them.

The rest made a circle under the tree and began to play. Jill was It first, and she tapped Carol. Karen and Connie tapped each other twice. Even if it was a little kids' game, they kept running and laughing.

Jill looked at Dede — part of the circle with everyone else. Nobody has tapped her yet, Jill thought. Next time I get the chance, I'll tap her and let her chase me. But in the end she didn't. She might fall down and get hurt, Jill told herself. But she'd chickened out and she knew it.

Next was tag.

"I can p-play tag," Dede told Lisa.

"Yeah?" said Lisa. "Well, I'm It. Got you!" And she tapped Dede's shoulder.

Dede grinned. She went after Marla, but Marla was too fast. Karen ran past. "G-got you!" yelled Dede.

"Dede! You're It?" Karen groaned.

"Yeh." Dede ran away behind the tree, laughing to beat the band.

During the game, Mom had the boys set up a long table and she put out sandwiches and cake and ice cream.

"Time to eat," she called out. "Your name cards will tell you where to sit."

Jill had printed Dede's name card big and put it next to her own place. Barney helped out. While everyone was looking for her seat, he ambled out of his spot under the bushes and sat down next to Jill. "Hey, Dede!" Jill shouted. "Barney's found your place for you!"

Dede was the last to leave the party. Jill said to her, "I'm going to help Mom clean up. She hasn't been feeling so great. You can get home okay with Barney, can't you?"

"Yeh." Dede nodded and smiled. "J-Jill . . ." Suddenly she put her arms around Jill and hugged her tight. "Y-you're my friend . . . I love you . . ."

Jill could hardly breathe. "Hey . . . Dede!" She wriggled free. "It's okay. I'm glad you had a good time."

"Yeh! I had a good time!"

"That's great. I'll see you."

Jill watched Dede go down the street. Even from the back you could tell she was smiling. Jill's arms still hurt from being hugged so hard. Nobody had ever told her "I love you" before — nobody but Mom and Dad anyway. Karen or Marla wouldn't say something like that. Probably they wouldn't feel it.

The weight of it came down on her. When someone loved you as much as that, it was something you couldn't fool around with.

Ten

The mellow fall suddenly turned nasty. The blue sky changed to gray and a raw wind blew down Maple. It bullied Squeak along the sidewalk. His tail streamed over his back like a flag at full stretch, the hairs parted neatly down the middle.

Jill tucked her free hand deep in the pocket of her windbreaker. The other, clamped around the leash, ached with cold and Jill studied it, fascinated by the pink and blue mottling.

"Come on, Squeak. Let's run!" she said. They raced the next three blocks, took the porch steps two at a time and burst into the kitchen. The warmth made Jill's nose run, and she sniffed deeply as she hung up her windbreaker.

There was a good smell coming from a pot

on the stove. Beef stew! She ran to the drawer for a spoon to taste the gravy. "Mmm!"

"Hey! I can hear you!" Mom's voice came from the living room. "Take it easy or there'll be nothing left"

Jill walked through to the living room. She said, "You wouldn't believe . . ." and stopped. "What *are* you doing?"

Mom was squatting on an exercise pad. "Exercises. I joined a class this morning. They have it in the Methodist Church basement. Special classes for pregnant women." She groaned. "O-o-h. I guess I've got a way to go!" She got up awkwardly. "What were you saying?"

"You wouldn't believe how cold it is out there, Mom. I can't stop sh-shaking. The wind goes right through my so-called windbreaker."

"I know. I nearly froze myself this morning. We've got to get organized and buy winter outfits." Mom shook her head. "I should've done it before this, but it's hard without the car. Maybe this weekend . . ."

"That'll be good."

"I don't know what Dad'll say." Mom sighed. "It's going to cost a fortune to get all of you what you need. We wouldn't have had to worry about it if we were still in California."

California. She hadn't thought about California for ages. How easy it was for a place you'd lived in all your life to just slip out of your mind.

Her mother interrupted her thoughts. "Stir the stew, honey." She was arching her back against her hand. "And maybe you can peel the carrots. Tom said he'd get to the potatoes as soon as he finished his math." She rubbed her back. "I'm pretty stiff. Maybe the exercises . . . I'll sit for a while."

"Sure. I'll make you some tea." Jill filled the kettle. "When can we get the winter stuff? Saturday morning?"

"I guess so. You'll have to get by till then. I hope it doesn't turn any colder. We'll go over to that big shopping center in Kellingford." She winced. "A-ah . . . that pain goes around the side and right down my leg . . ."

"I'll rub your back."

"Would you, Jilly? I really think it might help . . ." She closed her eyes and leaned forward on the table.

Jill rubbed just below her mother's thickened waist, where the ache seemed to be centered. She was sending a message with her hand to the baby inside. "I'm your big sister. I'm going to take care of you — and rock you — and sing to you — and you're going to love it here."

She felt her mother's taut muscles begin to relax. At almost the same moment, she felt a soft thump against her hand. She drew in her breath. The baby! Thump. Thump. "Message received!" That baby had to be okay!

All week the wind used Maple like a funnel, setting the loose shutters banging against the houses. As Jill and Dede walked the dogs one afternoon they watched a young man in a leather jacket putting up Mrs. Burns's storm windows. She was helping from inside, dressed for the cold weather in a fluffy pink sweater. "It feels like Alaska out there," she was saying. "You want to come in and have a hot drink?"

"You bet," he said.

She saw the girls and waved. "Want some cocoa? I'm just making some."

"Yeh," Dede said.

"We'd like to, but we can't," Jill answered. "We have to get home . . . Thanks anyway."

Mrs. Atkins was stacking logs on the porch when they got back and they helped her for a while. Shivering in her thin windbreaker, Jill dreamed of Saturday — Jacket Day.

"We're getting our winter clothes this weekend," she told Dede.

"Yeh?"

"I'm getting a red ski jacket."

"I l-like red."

"So do I. It's my favorite color."

"I h-have a ski jacket. It has a . . . h-hood."

"I want one with a hood, too."

"Yeh."

As Jill walked to school with Marla the next morning, she told her, "I'm getting a winter jacket tomorrow."

"Don't you have one?"

"We didn't need them in San Diego."

"No kidding."

"I think I'll get a red . . ."

"Hey, Karen — oo-hoo! Wait up, Karen! I have to tell you something . . ." Marla waved at Karen, walking a block ahead.

Jill shut up. If she doesn't want to listen, she thought, I'm not going to bother talking. Her excitement leaked away as she listened to Marla gab to Karen about going to Boston on Saturday and how it was for a special reason she couldn't talk about. Big deal!

Friday evening, Mom had a headache. "I don't know what he's going to say — those clothes are going to cost so much . . . Set the table, Jilly, while I make the chicken gravy." She stuffed some biscuits into the oven. "Dad'll be home any minute. I want to straighten my hair."

"He's here," said Jill. She always listened for the sound of the car in the street. She opened the door.

The wind blew him into the middle of the room. "Whew!" he said, grinning. "Some weather you folks are having!" He hugged them both. "How're my girls?" He studied Mom's face and kissed her cheek and twirled her around. "You look prettier every time I come home!" he said, and danced her around the room.

"Joe! Cut it out!" Mom laughed.

Dad's voice brought the boys downstairs. "Hey, Dad. What's happening?" Larry always tried to sound cool.

"What's happening? I'll tell you what's happening! Something special, that's what!"

"Joe!" Mom swept her hair back with her hands. "Calm down, for heaven's sakes! What is it?"

"Ta-da! The job in Pawnatucket is finished! We got through today and what's more — " he waved an envelope in the air — "we got a bonus for doing it ahead of schedule!"

"And the next job," Mom whispered.

"And the next job is at the woolen mills, here in York Falls."

He sat down and pulled Mom on to his lap, big as she was. "They're pleased with my work, Peg. After I lost that other job, I . . ."

Tears filled Mom's eyes. "Oh, Joe . . ."

He's been afraid all this time, Jill thought. Both of them have. She wanted to hug them, but they didn't know she was there any more.

* * *

Saturday they all went to the shopping center. Jill picked her jacket out of three racks full. It was *the* one — shiny red, puffy with dacron polyester filling, a hood you could zipper on or off or out of sight into its own hiding place, and plenty of pockets.

It was late afternoon when they got home and the lights were on at Marla's.

"She's back from Boston. I want to show her my jacket," Jill said, scrambling out of the car.

Mrs. Burns opened the door. "Well, hi there!" she said. "Come on in and join the party!"

"Party? Oh, I'm sorry . . . I just . . . I'll come back."

"No-o! Don't be silly, Jilly." She pulled Jill inside. "Silly Jilly — hey, I'm a poet and I don't know it! Isn't that right?" She smiled at a man sitting in a chair by the fire. "Me and my friend were just having a little pick-me-up after the trip from Boston. How 'bout you, silly Jilly?"

"Laraine!" Marla came into the room. Her face was red. "Laraine — I'll take Jill up to my room."

"O-kay. Have fun, hon." She laughed.

"Come on, Jill," Marla said.

When they were upstairs, Jill said, "Who's that? Al?"

"No. His name's Morton Tanzhandler. He's her agent. He's trying to get her some work around here."

"Oh. Boy, I'd like to see her dance!"

"How about me?" Marla's voice was sharp. "Don't you want to see me dance?"

"Sure I do. I'd love to see you dance, Marla."

"Okay."

Jill twirled around. "Notice anything?"

"You got a winter jacket."

"Yes. Isn't it neat? Look at the pockets and the crest on the shoulder. Don't you love it? It's really warm — I wore it home to test it out."

"It's a very nice jacket, Jill," Marla said. Then her eyes lit up. "Look at what my grandma got me in Boston!"

The bed was covered with clothes. Corduroy gauchos. A long print skirt with a peasant blouse. A white angora sweater. And a ski jacket. Brilliant royal blue. A ski patch already sewn on each shoulder. Pockets everywhere. A hood, framed in soft white fur. And white fur mittens lying beside it.

"Oh!" Jill had never seen anything so beautiful.

"It's goosedown. That's the warmest you can get, you know. Much warmer than an ordinary polyester filling. It'll keep me warm at 60 degrees below."

Jill thought, I'd like to see you somewhere where it's 60 degrees below.

"The mittens and hood are real fur." Marla rubbed a glove against Jill's cheek. "Feel it —

isn't that divine! My grandma says furs and jewels should always be the real thing."

"Yes. They . . . they're really great, Marla. You're the best-dressed kid in sixth grade, that's for sure . . . Well. I have to be going . . ."

"Oh. Do you? Can't you stay awhile? What did you come over for?"

"Nothing special. I'll see you, Marla."

Jill let herself out. She didn't want to go home. Mom would ask what Marla had said about the jacket and then she'd drag out some wise old saying about not judging a book by its cover or handsome is as handsome does. She couldn't stand hearing that right now.

She put her head down against the wind, the red hood drawn around her face, and marched down Maple feeling mad.

"H-hi, Jill." Dede and Barney were crossing Elm, coming toward her.

"Oh. Hi."

Dede pointed toward Jill's house. "We were c-coming to see you."

"You were? We've been in Kellingford buying winter clothes. See? I got my jacket,"

"I l-like that!" Dede's smile broadened. "It's red. I like that." She touched the sleeve. "I like it, Jill. P-pockets. Th-that's good. Pockets are g-good."

"There're a zillion of them. It's part of why I picked this one. There's a pocket for change.

And one for a ski-lift ticket or a bus ticket or something. And side pockets for mittens . . . even some inside. Look!"

She unzipped the jacket. The wind whipped in. "Brr!" She shivered and did it up in a hurry. Warmth surrounded her again. It *was* a great jacket, whether Marla thought so or not.

"Why were you coming over now?" Jill asked. "It's dark. You should be home."

"I w-want to ask you something. I c-couldn't wait." Dede smiled. There was a silence.

After a moment Jill said, "Well? What?"

"Oh. Yeh. Uh . . . w-we're having a Christmas party at school. We can ask a f-friend. So I want to ask you. You asked m-me to your party. You're my f-friend."

Eleven

"I can't go. I can't." Jill heard her voice rise.

"Nobody's making you, Jilly," Dad said quietly. "What did you tell her?"

"I . . . I said I'd have to ask and I'd let her know."

"When is it?"

"The Saturday before Christmas."

"There'll be a lot going on then," Mom said.

"I know and I'll probably be very busy . . ."

"We'll talk about this later. Let's eat now. Dinner's getting cold," Dad said.

It was a quiet meal. Everyone concentrated hard on eating and a heavy silence blanketed the table, broken only by the clatter of their forks. Jill was trying to get rid of the picture filling her mind — the faces in the windows of Dede's school bus.

She pushed her plate away. "I don't want any more," she said. "I have some homework. Can I be excused?"

Mom nodded. "Clear your place . . . And, honey, we'll work something out."

Jill climbed the stairs slowly, hearing conversation break out in relief as soon as she left the room. She undressed and stretched out on her bed in the dark. From time to time, a car whooshed by and the headlights made shadows along her wall.

Dad came up after a while. "How's it going, baby?"

"I don't know what to do."

"I know."

"Either way, it'll be bad. I mean, if I don't go, I know she'll be disappointed and I'll feel terrible about letting her down. But if I do go . . . oh, Dad . . . if you want to know the truth . . . I'm scared to go."

"I remember you telling me a while back that Karen was scared of Dede."

"Yes. But I know Dede. And anyway, Dede's much better than most of them. You should see them, Dad. I've seen them on her bus. They're gross. Some are all twisted and some are blind and some have to wear helmets . . ."

"That's really gross all right."

"Oh, Dad." She was ashamed. "I can't help how I feel."

"I don't mean to make fun of you, Jilly. But I do think you're letting yourself be spooked by the idea of going because you don't really know what to expect when you get there."

"That's it! I mean . . . what can a bunch like that do at a party? They can't even talk so you can understand, some of them . . ." Panic rose again, smothering her words.

"Can you guess how hard it must be for them — trying to say something and having nobody understand? Wouldn't it make you mad?"

"Yes. I guess so. But suppose I do try, and I still don't understand? Then I'll say 'Excuse me?' and then they'll say it over, and it'll sound just the same and I'll say 'Excuse me?' again . . ."

Dad nodded. He stared at the dark wall. Then he said, "You know, they always say that the worst fear of all is fear of the unknown. . . Think things over, honey. You'll figure out what's best." He patted her shoulder, sighed, and left her.

All day Sunday, the decision she had to make weighed like something heavy growing inside her. It loomed in her thoughts, putting everything else out of focus. It deadened the day.

Monday, she saw Dede in the distance and ducked down a side street, feeling like a criminal.

Tuesday was worse. Marla did a really funny imitation of the janitor and she couldn't even smile. She kept losing track of what she was doing in class and Mr. Lopietro yelled at her.

"What's with you?" Karen asked on the way home.

Jill just shook her head. She didn't want to tell them. Oh, they'd say right off how gross it was and of course she wasn't going and it'd be the same story all over again. Everyone ganging up against old Dede — Jill Harvey, her so-called friend, included.

Jill sipped her hot chocolate by the fire. Mom sat in the chair opposite and stared at the flames. Her face was sad and inward-looking, the way she looked whenever she was thinking about the baby. Now Jill knew how it felt, having fear lodged inside you. Mom had almost three months to wait.

Jill took a deep breath and got up from the table.

"I'm taking Squeak for a walk," she said.

"Dress warm," her mother said.

Dress warm for your trip to the unknown, Jill thought, zipping up her red jacket.

She climbed the steps to Dede's house and

rang the bell. She knew Dede would be out. It was her day to swim at the Y.

"Hi, Jill, come on in. I'm just having a cup of coffee," Mrs. Atkins said. "What can I get you? Coke? Milk?" She was too welcoming.

"Nothing, thanks. Mrs. Atkins. . ."

"Well, at least sit down here by the fire for a moment. I see Squeak's already found himself a spot." She nudged Jill into a chair. "So! What's on your mind? I don't often see you on Tuesdays."

"I know." Jill sat on the edge of the armchair. "Mrs. Atkins . . ." She felt her face going red. "I . . . I wonder if you could tell me what it's like at . . . at Dede's school?"

"What it's . . . why, it's real nice. It's a new building and it's light and airy — lots of windows — and everything painted fresh and bright."

"Oh."

"That's not what you meant. Is it?"

"No." Jill stared at her hands and then looked up, feeling almost defiant. Why did she have to feel so guilty about asking. "I need to know, Mrs. Atkins. About the . . . other kids."

Mrs. Atkins lit a cigarette. "I knew Dede was going to ask you to the party. She was so all fired up about it she couldn't sleep the night before." She leaned forward. "It's the first time she's had a friend to ask, you know. It means a lot to her."

"I'm sorry, Mrs. Atkins," she said, not looking at her. "I need to know."

"Yes." Mrs. Atkins got up and poured herself another cup of coffee. "I can see how the idea of all those children together might make you nervous if you weren't used to them." She settled back into her chair. "There are a whole lot of those kids at Dede's school — it's shocking to see so many, so many. . . They're disabled in many ways. But the teachers put the classes together according to what they can do rather than by age or handicap, so it works out pretty well."

"But how do they get that way?"

"Oh, honey . . . it can happen for so many reasons. There's Down's syndrome," Mrs. Atkins said. "What Dede has. That's the result of an extra set of chromosomes in each cell in her body — it's like Mother Nature made a mistake in her arithmetic." Mrs. Atkins smiled faintly. "Then there are the kids who have spina bifida. That happens when things don't get put together right before the baby's born and there's damage to the spinal chord. Lots of times kids like that are paralyzed, so they're in wheelchairs."

Jill pulled Squeak to her.

"Some of the older children at the school

are PKU kids. whose brains were damaged as tiny babies because their bodies were missing a certain enzyme. A way to test for that has been discovered and now most babies are checked out as soon as they're born. There's a special diet for PKU kids that'll prevent brain damage, but that discovery came too late for the kids at Dede's school."

The fire was dying down. Mrs. Atkins put another log on. "Have a Coke or something to keep me company?" she said.

"Okay."

They went into the kitchen and Mrs. Atkins opened a can of soda. "There're ice cubes in the freezer, honey. Do you want to hear more?"

"Yes."

"Well, some of the kids are retarded because their mothers had German measles before their babies were born. Then sometimes a baby will be fine right up to the moment of birth, when something happens to cut the oxygen supply to its brain. It only takes a little lapse to cause brain damage. . . Sometimes disabled children have a whole lot of things go wrong at once — blindness and deafness, maybe epilepsy, too — on top of the retardation. Dede's one of the lucky ones, believe it or not."

They went back to the fire. Jill tried to imagine what they looked like, all those kids, all those different things wrong with them, all together in one big room.

"I still can't figure out what they do in school. I don't see what they *can* do!" she said.

"You'd be surprised. I'm going to be straight with you. Some are at a very low level. I mean, they're still learning to go to the bathroom by themselves. And some of them can't even do that and have to be taken every half hour by an aide."

"You mean the little kids."

"Age doesn't have anything to do with it. One of the boys is eighteen, I think. Dede's age."

"Dede's . . .? You mean Dede's eighteen?" Jill couldn't keep the shock out of her face.

Mrs. Atkins said quickly, "But some of the others are learning to read and write and do simple arithmetic, so they can make change, things like that. And they do arts and crafts. Dede wove this little coaster here. And gym and homemaking — you know, ironing, cleaning, simple cooking. And some are beginning to learn a job, so they can go to a sheltered workshop later and earn a little money. There's a lot they can do. More than people give them credit for." She pushed a candy box at Jill. "Have one, honey. You don't have to worry about your figure, do you? You know, the school has put Dede on a diet!" She laughed nervously. "Just when I'd promised her we'd be baking Christmas cookies soon!" She stabbed at the fire with the poker. "This Christmas party is their big chance to show their families and friends around. They look forward to it very much. They want to demonstrate what they've been learning for the Special Olympics for the handicapped."

"Dede talked about it once. But I thought she meant . . . well . . . I just thought. . ."

"I know. Nobody thinks they can do anything. But they can. It takes them a long time and they have to work real hard at it. But they can do a lot, if people'll just understand and give them a chance."

Jill stared at the fire. Mrs. Atkins leaned forward in her chair, her eyes urgent.

"I'd drive you up there, Jill . . . and drive you home afterward."

"You'll be there too?"

"Sure. The whole time. I'm taking some of the food. I'll be right there with you. . ."

"I hadn't thought about that. Of course you'll be there." Jill laughed with relief. "And there'll be all the other mothers and other friends. . ."

"Sure. You won't be alone. And my Dede'll be there. She'll look after you."

Twelve

Jill threw down the paste pot. "Look at that!" she said. "It's sliding sideways. I pasted it straight and it's sliding sideways!" She stared at her model of a Greek theater, which was subsiding before her eyes on its cardboard base. "I hate projects! I've been working on this for two hours and now it's self-destructing, stupid thing!" She pushed her chair back. "I refuse to do any more to it. I'm going out!"

Mom grinned. "You could do with a breather. Take Squeak. He's getting fat again. You've been shortchanging him on walks now that it's colder."

Jill put on her jacket and pulled the hood around her face. Squeak came running at the jingle of the leash and they set off down Maple, walking fast. They could make a better pace without Dede. It felt good to really stretch out. Dede was home with a cold so she and Barney hadn't walked with them for a couple of days. Mrs. Atkins said she was keeping Dede in "for safety's sake."

The street was empty. Jill breathed the cold air deep into her lungs and felt exhilarated, alive all over. They passed windows lit against the early darkness and she saw people moving in the rooms behind, but it seemed to her that only she was real and they were moving pictures on a TV screen.

Something touched her forehead. Reaching up, she found nothing. The bare branches clattered against each other as a sudden wind gusted through. Once again, something. She looked up. A white feather drifted down. Then, as she followed its fall out of the sky, it was as if some giant far above suddenly ripped open a bolster and shook it over the world. A million trillion feathers came tumbling all at once from the sky, frosting Squeak's tail and the bare branches and the narrow gabled roofs of the houses. Jill turned her face up to receive her first snow and began to whirl like a crazy thing.

"I love it! I love it!" she sang. And Squeak yipped and squealed and ran in circles, too, until his leash got tangled around Jill's legs and finally brought them to a stop. But the sky and the snow and the houses on Maple continued whirling.

She ran back up the street.

"Marla!" she yelled under Marla's window. "Come out! It's snowing!"

Marla stuck her head out. "Hey, great"

Her head disappeared and, after a few moments, she ran down her steps in her royal blue down jacket with the white fur hood.

"I told Laraine," Marla said. "All she said was 'Oh, for Pete's sake! I'll have to put the snow tires on.' "

They laughed.

"Want to walk to the schoolyard and back?" Jill asked.

"Sure."

Everything was quiet. The snow had settled down to a steady fall.

Jill ran for the swings when they got to the schoolyard. "I love to swing." She laughed a little. "I'm too big to use them in school time." She pumped her legs, going higher and higher until she was flying with the snowflakes — so high that the swing chains began to tremble.

"You'd better come down before you fall off," Marla called.

"Uh-uh."

"Come down."

"Why don't you swing?"

"Because I don't want to. There's snow all

over the seat. I don't want to get wet." Marla stared up at Jill. "I'll tell you something if you come down. Something I haven't told anyone yet, not even Karen."

"What is it?"

Marla dug her toe in the snow. "Well. Maybe I shouldn't. It's nothing really. I'd better not."

"Marla Burns! You fink!" Jill jumped off the swing.

"I was trying to save your life, dum-dum."

"Don't pull that. I can tell there's something. . ."

Marla grinned and then her face went serious. "Okay. But I'm swearing you to secrecy!"

"Okay."

"It's the biggest thing that's ever happened in my entire life!"

"I believe you! What *is* it?

"Well, okay. All that's happened is . . . I got picked to dance in *The Nutcracker* in Boston!"

"You . . . I don't believe it!"

"I know. Neither do I! I went to audition a couple of weekends ago. I never would've had the nerve, but my grandma made me. Then I was called back and we heard for sure today."

"Oh, Marla. . ."

"I have to rehearse every day from now on. Laraine's driving me to Boston in the morning.

I have to live at my grandma's until the run is over."

"The run?"

"The run of the ballet. That's what they call it. There're going to be eleven performances."

"What about school?"

"They said I could go. I have to do an extra paper about the ballet — the story and the music and how it is to work on stage and what it's like backstage. And they're going to send me work and I have to send it back by mail. And I have to do extra reading. It's only for four weeks though — two weeks rehearsing, then the show, I guess they figure I won't get too far behind. Anyway. What do I care if I do?" She pirouetted across the playground. "But I've left the best for last. . ."

"What?" Jill ran after her.

"You're all coming to the opening."

"Who?"

"You. And Karen. And Connie. My grandma's so excited she said I could ask my best friends to see my debut. She's inviting you to sleep over at her apartment."

"Marla — don't kid around."

"I'm *not* — she's arranging the whole thing."

Jill's head whirled. "I've never been to a real ballet. You know, professional. And in Boston!

I've wanted to go to Boston ever since we moved here."

Marla laughed. "And there I'll be — right up there on the stage! Then you'll come?"

"Will I! Try and stop me! When is it?"

"The Saturday before Christmas."

Thirteen

Jill started taking Squeak on a new route.

"It's boring going the same old way all the time," she said, "so now I go up Maple instead of down, then across Butternut, down Acacia and back across Elm."

"You mean you're not going by Dede's any more?" Mom asked.

"No."

"Dede'll miss walking with you."

Jill pulled open the hall closet door. "She . . . doesn't go out so much in this cold weather." She tugged at her jacket. "This stupid zipper! It's always sticking on this stupid jacket!" she said, her voice shaking. "Anyway . . . well . . . well, I don't see why it has to be always me who has to walk with Dede all the time."

111

"Why, Jilly! You told me you liked walking with her."

"I *do*! Only . . . oh, quit bugging me!"

"You don't have to snap."

"I'm not snapping. Just leave me alone."

"Gladly."

Jill stamped up the stairs to her room. She lay on her bed and opened her science book. They had to read the whole chapter and then do the examples at the end. But as Marla said, who cares? I don't care either, Jill thought, banging the book shut. I'm not going to be a scientist. She lay on her back and stared at the ceiling.

She was still staring at the ceiling an hour later when Dad came home. She heard him greet Mom and whistle as he hung his coat up. Why did he have to whistle all the time! That's all he ever did nowadays, whistle, whistle, whistle.

Larry and Tom came slamming into the house.

"What's for dinner?" Larry yelled. He always yelled after hockey practice.

"Hamburgers," Mom answered. "And I need the table set."

Jill listened to them down there, laughing and talking. After a while, she heard Dad say, "Where's my girl?" and a few moments later he came up the stairs two at a time.

"Here you are," he said.

Well! That's pretty obvious, she thought.

112

"Doing your homework?" He sat on the bed.

"No."

"Oh . . . What's the matter?"

"Nothing."

"Come off it, Jilly. This is your old dad talking. What's going on in that head of yours? Your mother says you're in a bad mood."

"I'm fine."

"You could've fooled me!"

Why doesn't he go away? she thought. He's always poking around in my mind. It isn't any of his business how I feel.

He stood up and wandered around the room, flipping through a book on her shelf, looking at the pictures on her Led Zeppelin album.

He broke the heavy silence. "What did Dede say?"

"When?"

"When you told her?"

"I haven't."

"Jilly!"

"I know! I just . . . haven't seen her around, that's all. I'll *do* it."

Dad sat down on the bed again. "Do you want us to?" His voice was gentle.

If only you could, she thought. But she said, "No. She wouldn't understand . . . hearing it from you . . ." She stared miserably at the wall. "Oh, Dad. Why did it have to turn out this way? Of all stupid days in the year!"

"It's a darn shame all right."

"I won't miss the chance to go to Boston. And I *can't* miss the ballet!"

"I know."

"I'll never get another chance like it!"

"I know."

I know, I know . . . is that all he could say?

The next day, a postcard came from Marla: *Dear Jill — I'm having a fabulous time. Boston is fabulous and I've got a fabulous costume to wear. Wait till you see it! Love, Marla.*

Late that afternoon, Jill went to Dede's.

"Come on in, honey," Mrs. Atkins said. "Turn the TV off, Dede. Jill's here."

The fire was blazing and the room was warm and cozy. Barney sniffed her hand in welcome, tail waving. Dede came out of the den.

"Hi, Jill. Want to w-watch TV?"

"No. I can't stay today, Dede. I just came because I have to tell you something. . ."

Dede smiled. Her face was wide open.

Jill thought, I can't. But she knew if she didn't it would still be waiting. Better to get it over.

"Dede — I'm sorry, but I can't come to your Christmas party after all."

The smile stayed on Dede's face.

"You see, I really thought I could come and I know it'll be fun and I'm real sorry about it. . ."

"Well, we're real sorry too. Aren't we, Dede?" Mrs. Atkins' voice was high and polite.

"What it is, Mrs. Atkins, is that I . . . I was going to be invited to Boston for the same day . . . only I didn't know about it when I said. . ."

"Sure. We quite understand. Don't we, Dede?" Mrs. Atkins was smiling. All except her eyes.

"It's true, Mrs. Atkins. You can ask my mother."

"Sure. Now, if you'll excuse us, Dede and I were just about to have our supper."

"Dede . . . I'm sorry. . ."

Dede nodded. "I know," she said. "It's okay." But now her smile was gone.

Jill walked home.

When she came in, she felt Dad looking at her, a question in his eyes. She nodded and shrugged her shoulders. Question answered.

"Get all your clothes packed tonight," Mom said on Friday. "Don't leave it till morning. You know how you are in the morning!"

"You already told me a hundred times!"

"Lay it all out on your bed and I'll come and make sure you haven't forgotten anything."

Jill laid out her yellow and brown dress. Probably the last time I'll wear it, she thought. It was a bit tight and Mom had had to let down the hem. Next to it, she spread her yellow sweater and blue pants, her pajamas, her robe and slippers, a change of underwear. She put *The Nutcracker* on the phonograph and tried to hum along while she got out her hairbrush and toothbrush and two pairs of socks.

Mom called her downstairs to the phone.

It was Connie. "Are you packed yet? Don't forget extra money for souvenirs. . . Are you taking a camera?"

"I'm not packing till later . . . don't have a camera . . . See you."

She hung up and went to get a suitcase from the attic. The phone rang again. It was Karen. "Should I take my mother's opera glasses? Did Marla say how far we'll be from the stage? Maybe we'll need the opera glasses. What do you think?"

"I don't know . . . she didn't tell me . . . maybe you should."

Jill stared at the suitcase open on her bed. The phone rang a third time.

Mom called, "For you, Jill. Hurry, honey. It's long distance."

Jill picked up the phone slowly. A whispery little voice at the other end said, "Hi! This is your friendly neighborhood ballet dancer calling."

"Hi, Marla."

"Are you all set? Laraine's picking you up at eight-thirty tomorrow morning. Oh, you're going to love it! You can't believe how fabulous it is. Wait till you see my costume — it's pink and it has silver spangles and when I'm under the lights I look fabulous! Grandma told me. She's been sneaking into the rehearsals and then working with me afterward to improve my dance. We've even put in a couple of little extras — you know, difficult steps — because she says this is a real showcase for me. The director didn't notice, isn't that a gas! . . . Jill . . . Are you there?"

"Yes. I'm here."

"Well, I may not be able to see you after the show because I have to go to a cast party at this fabulous restaurant. But Grandma said she'd get the teenager who lives in the next apartment to take you home after the show. We'll be driven over in this big limousine, can you imagine! . . . Yes, Grandma, I *am* hurrying. . ."

"Marla. . ."

"And Grandma bought me a new dress for the party which is just . . ."

Marla's voice chattered on in Jill's ear. But it was Dede's face that filled her mind.

"Marla. . ."

"What?"

"I'm not coming."

Silence at the other end. Then, "I didn't hear what you said."

"I said I'm not coming. I'm sorry, Marla. You

know I want to. But . . . well, something's happened here, and . . . well, there's something else I have to do instead."

"What do you mean? It's all set up. You've got to."

"Maybe you could give the ticket to someone else."

"You mean you're serious? You're really not coming? But I've told everyone here you're my best friend . . . you, not Karen . . . and that you're just dying to see me in the show. If you don't come, what'll they think? They'll laugh at me. You've got to come, Jill. I need you to come. Jill, it's my first big show. . ." Marla's voice sounded far off. "Jill? Why aren't you coming? Tell me! What's so important? What is it you have to do?"

"Well . . . what happened was Dede had asked me to this party at her school. . ."

"That retard?"

"Yes. They're having a Christmas party and she was counting on me going and I had told her yes before you. . ."

Marla's voice rose. "What's the matter with you? Are you crazy? You're going to pass up a chance to see me in a professional show, just to go to some dumb party with her? She'll never know the difference. But I will . . . Please come, Jill. Please. I really am petrified, Jill. I need my friends out there."

"Dede needs a friend, too. You've got Karen and Connie, but she hasn't got anyone else but me. Marla, I can't let her down."

"What about letting me down! And I came to your stupid party for her — you owe me for that, Jill Harvey, and you know it. . ."

"I'm sorry. It's just that . . ."

"Okay. Forget it. And you can forget you're my friend from now on, Jill Harvey. I think you're a creep. Just like your creepy friend!"

Far away in Boston, Marla slammed down the phone. Jill listened to the hum of the empty wire. She felt light. Like . . . bread rising. . . Very gently she hung up the phone. Laughing and crying, she ran to the kitchen.

"Mom! Hey, Mom! I'm going over to Dede's for a couple of minutes!"

Fourteen

Jill settled Mrs. Atkins' chocolate cake more squarely on her lap and stared ahead as the car started climbing the long approach to the Pearson School. Funny how all the schools here in the East seemed to be at the top of hills. Maybe the people in charge thought it was healthier. She tried to follow that thought, so she wouldn't think about what lay ahead. But the tight feeling in her stomach stayed right where it was.

"Good luck, honey," Dad had said. "You'll do fine."

Easy for him to say. He'd never faced a school full of retarded kids. Come to that, Jill thought, I bet nobody I know has.

They reached the top of the hill. Jill swallowed, trying to moisten her dry throat. Mrs.

Atkins pulled into a parking space and got out briskly. Oh, couldn't we wait a minute? Jill thought. But Mrs. Atkins had already come around to her side of the car.

"I'll take the cake, Jill. You bring that box of sandwiches from the back seat."

She followed Mrs. Atkins toward the low buildings. There were Christmas decorations on the windows. Jill had expected bars.

The flag in front of the building whipped in the wind, its line beating a tattoo against its steel pole.

"That wind's raw," Mrs. Atkins said. "I wish it would warm up — Dede's getting a cold. Ordinarily I'd have made her stay in today, but I didn't have the heart — she's been looking forward to this party so much."

Mrs. Atkins headed for a side door and motioned Jill in front of her.

She was inside. The door closed behind her. Why aren't I in Boston? she thought. She looked carefully around, trying not to catch anyone's eye, trying not to show she was curious. She imagined someone waltzing up to her and saying, "Do you come here often?" the way they did in the movies. She felt giggles rising crazily inside her.

"We'll take this stuff to the kitchen," Mrs. Atkins said. Jill followed her down a corridor, staying close. "You see, honey, it's not so very different from your school, is it?"

Jill shook her head. What had she expected? Chains — locks — awful noises? What she saw was bulletin boards, classrooms with tables, blackboards, pianos. . .

They came to an open space, separated by shelving.

"See, this is their kitchen," Mrs. Atkins said. "They've got everything here they'd find in a standard kitchen. This is where they learn to cook, wash dishes, put stuff away properly . . ."

Jill nodded.

Next to the kitchen was a kind of sitting room, with couches and chairs, a TV and a phonograph.

"The kids take breaks in here," Mrs. Atkins said, "and the staff uses it to teach them about correct behavior when they're with other people — you know, in a social situation. Also they practice their household skills here — dusting, polishing, vacuuming. . ."

Jill nodded. She knew she hadn't spoken a word since they'd entered the building. She had to *say* something. "Uh . . . Dede must know more than I do about how to do those things," she said.

"Right!" Mrs. Atkins beamed at her. "Now look over here, Jill. This is their supermarket area."

Cans of soup and vegetables, packets of cereals and tea and pet food lined the shelves on both sides of an aisle.

"Here the kids learn how to stack the shelves neatly, with everything right side up. Some of them might get jobs in a supermarket later on. And they learn how to shop — pick stuff out — recognize labels even if they can't read. It helps them to be more useful to themselves and their families. They feel good when they can be self-sufficient, and it's even better when they can share in the work of the family."

"Yes," Jill said.

A boy was coming toward them. His head was too big for his body, and his tiny round ears stuck out like cup handles. Jill slipped around to the other side of Mrs. Atkins.

"Hi, Mrs. Atkins," the boy said in a slow, deep voice.

"Hi, Donald. How are you today?"

"I'm f-fine, Mrs. Atkins. How are you today?"

"Just fine, thank you, Donald."

The boy went on by and Jill realized she'd been holding her breath. Supposing he'd talked to me? she thought. It's easy for Mrs. Atkins — she's used to them.

They left the food in the kitchen. "Let's find Dede," Mrs. Atkins said.

The corridor was empty. Mrs. Atkins put her

arm around Jill's shoulder. "It's not too bad, is it?"

Jill shook her head. But she couldn't bring herself to come right out and say it. Mrs. Atkins gave her a squeeze. "They'll be waiting in the gym."

Jill could hear voices and laughter as they got closer. A girl who looked like Dede overtook them, pushing a wheelchair with a small boy in it. His body was propped like a rag doll, legs dangling. He was laughing fit to bust. After they'd passed, Jill realized she was smiling. She felt her stomach begin to ease.

The gym was just like hers at York Falls Elementary. They play basketball? she thought, staring at the court laid out in red on the polished wood floor. There were windows high on the walls and equipment stacked neatly at one end of the gym. Students and parents were everywhere. But not many kids like me, Jill thought, looking warily around.

"H-hi, Jill!" Dede touched her arm. "I knew you'd c-come!"

"Hey, Dede! You have a nice school"

"Yeh. I l-like it" Dede said. "Let's s-sit down over here." She led the way and they sat down next to a big blond girl in a blue dress.

"Hi, babe!" she greeted Jill. A pretty weird way to say hello! Jill thought.

Dede said, "Jill, th-this is my very g-good friend, Debbie."

It sounded . . . funny . . . formal. She'd never heard Dede talk that way. She didn't know how to answer. She looked at Mrs. Atkins. Mrs. Atkins was nodding encouragement.

"Uh, hi, Debbie. Uh, my name is Jill."

Debbie said, "Sit down."

They already were, but Jill said, "Thank you." She felt like Alice in Wonderland. Everything was just a bit . . . off center.

A lot of the students looked like Dede. Quite a few others wore football helmets.

"Is that the boy that goes on your bus, Dede?" Jill looked at someone near them. "I saw a boy in a helmet on your bus."

"Th-that's David. G-George goes on my bus."

"Why does he wear a helmet?"

"He f-falls down sometimes."

"Oh . . . yeah," Jill said.

Mrs. Atkins said, "David has epilepsy."

Suppose he has an attack right here in front of us, Jill thought. She watched him, fascinated — half afraid it would happen, half hoping it would, so she could see what it would be like.

"Good afternoon." A woman spoke from the far end of the gym. "I'm Barbara Lanz. I'm pleased to welcome all of you to the Pearson Christmas party. Today, our students are going to show you the school and what we can do. We hope you enjoy yourselves. Thank you for coming."

"C-come on, Jill," Dede said, grabbing her arm. "We go this way w-with Mrs. L-Linner." She pulled Jill toward a large, dark woman.

"Is she your teacher?"

"Yeh! Sh-she's nice!"

Mrs. Linner led her group of students and parents through some locker rooms to the swimming pool.

"You're lucky!" Jill said. "We don't have a pool at York Falls."

They watched some kids jumping from a low diving board into the water. One after the other, they went off the board like frogs, came bobbing to the surface and swam to the side. At the end of the line, a boy about eight clung to the teacher. "No!" he wailed. He was crying, shaking his head, his tears flying in different directions.

"Th-that's Freddie," Dede said.

"Are they going to make him do it?" Jill said. "It isn't high."

"But he doesn't want to . . ."

"F-Freddie doesn't like water."

"He's so afraid."

"He always does that."

They watched as the other students and teachers crowded around Freddie, trying to talk him into it. After a while, he must have realized there was no way out. He walked to the end of the board. I know how he feels, Jill thought. He jumped off. A teacher was waiting in the water and swam with him to the side.

"You see, Freddie. You *can* do it!" the teacher said, boosting him out of the water. "That was good!"

"Yeah!" Freddie strutted out to the end of the board again.

"Let's move on to the workroom," Mrs. Linner said. They followed her along a hallway to an area where different projects were laid out on benches. A couple of students stood by.

"That's Harold," Dede told Jill, pointing to a thin boy. "Hi-hi, Harold! And that's Mary. Sh-she's my friend. Hi, Mary!"

Harold didn't reply, but Mary said, "Hi, Dede."

Mrs. Linner lined them up so everyone could see the work in progress. "Mary prints custom-made matchbook covers on this press here," she said. Mary lifted the printing lever, placed a plain silver cover down on the plate beneath, and then brought the lever down sharply on top of it. She lifted it and picked out the matchbook cover so everyone could see what she had done. The initials *MD* in crimson stood out on the silver. "Mary will be glad to fill your orders for Christmas, bar mitzvahs, silver weddings, any festive occasion . . ." Mrs. Linner smiled. "That's very good, Mary."

"Harold here . . ." Mrs. Linner looked around. Harold was hiding behind Mary. "It's okay, Harold," Mrs. Linner said. She pulled him out gently. "No need to hide — we're all friends today." She looked at her audience. "Harold has had some unhappy experiences with strangers." The boy stood awkwardly in front of everyone, staring at the floor. He doesn't look retarded, Jill thought. He just looks shy. He must hate everyone staring at him.

"Harold is a whiz at counting," Mrs. Linner said. "So he counts the matchbook covers for Mary and packs them into boxes of fifty. He hasn't made a mistake in six months." Harold smiled at the floor. "Harold and Mary will be graduating soon. Then they'll be going to the sheltered workshop every day. They can earn money there doing some of the things they've learned here."

Mrs. Linner led them through the kitchen and supermarket areas and into a classroom where ten little kids were sitting in a circle, singing and clapping their hands. Every time the verse ended, a different child got up, turned around, and said his or her name.

In the middle of the song, a teacher's aide very quietly took one of the kids by the hand and walked out of the room. Bathroom, Jill thought. A while later, they came back. "Hi, P-Paula," Dede said. The aide led Paula back to her chair and then marked a chart on the wall.

One of the kids began running around. She looked quite a bit like Marla, except for the slant to her big blue eyes.

Her teacher said, "Sit down, please, Charlene."

Charlene sat down, only in front of one of the others, making faces at him. All the kids started laughing and making faces. The teacher didn't say anything. She didn't get mad. But she picked Charlene up off the floor like a doll and popped her into a bin in the corner so tall that she disappeared. Jill gasped. She waited for howls from the bin. But there wasn't a sound.

Mrs. Linner beckoned the group out of the room.

"Charlene hasn't been here very long," she said. "When she came to us, she'd been very spoiled — everyone at her home did everything for her and she's used to being the center of attention. She's learning not to disturb the class, but sometimes she forgets." She smiled at Jill. "Don't worry. Her teacher will take her out in a minute, as soon as she settles down."

Jill turned. "Dede . . ."

Mrs. Atkins said, "She's gone to change. We'll catch up with her in the gym."

The gym was full of students dressed in navy blue shorts and white shirts. The gym teacher blew his whistle. "I want to explain to our visitors that we are training for the Special Olympics in the spring, a day of sports events for the handicapped. Everyone can go — the idea is to take part — but we try to do the best we can by training hard. To help us, we're lucky enough to have a group of seventh graders who come regularly from Kellingford Middle School to work with our students."

Jill stared at the helpers. They were only a year older than she was. Imagine coming to a place like this and working with the kids! They were like . . . professionals.

The helpers were grinning and fooling around with the students. They didn't look a bit scared of them. I would, she thought. I'd be scared to death to try to teach them anything. Well . . . not Dede, of course . . . but then I know her, so that's different.

The gym teacher spoke again. "The first thing we'll do is run to the wall at the end of the gym and back again." He blew his whistle and the kids began running. Some went fine. Some fell down. Some didn't move.

"Come on, Margaret. You can run!" a helper urged. Margaret stood still, frowning. "I'll hold your hand and we'll run together," the helper said. Margaret shook her head. Another helper said, "I know what she wants. She wants us to swing her, like last time!" Margaret smiled. Holding hands, the three of them began to run along together and, when they got going fast enough, the two helpers swung Margaret up between them, while she laughed and cried, "Again!"

"Now, pay attention!" the gym teacher said. "You're going to start out running. But when I blow my whistle, you're going to stop and crouch. Then when I blow again, you're going to get up and start running again. Okay. Let's try that!" He blew his whistle. Some of the kids ran. But some crouched instead of running. One boy near Jill began to cry. Jill thought, he doesn't know which to do. But his helper said, "It's okay, Pete. That's hard. We'll practice it together." The boy stopped crying.

"Next, we're going to roll along the floor," the teacher called. He demonstrated by getting down on the floor himself and everyone laughed as he rolled over and over like a log in water. Some of the kids were rolled along by their helpers because they couldn't do it by themselves.

Jill was watching some kids clustered around a girl lying on the floor. "Roll, Dawn!" they said. She squeezed her eyes shut. "We'll roll you," they said. She shook her head and jammed her thumb into her mouth. The teacher came up.

"Hey, Dawn, you sunbathing or something?" In a moment he had her laughing and on her feet. He didn't make her roll and Jill was glad. "Dawn says she'll try for me tomorrow," the teacher said. He patted her shoulder and turned to help a girl whose student was stamping his foot and screaming. "Rob, no!" he said, sharply. "You must not do that! Bad!" A seventh grader near Jill whispered, "Rob bites when he gets mad." She sounded matter-of-fact about it.

Her friend said, "I'd be scared to work with him."

"I know. So would I. But Irene really loves him. She visits him at the home. His family never goes to see him."

Jill glanced at Mrs. Atkins.

"It's hard for him," Mrs. Atkins said. "He feels mad inside and he doesn't know how to tell anyone. The teachers understand. But they have to help him manage his feelings."

Jill looked back at Rob. He was crying now. The gym teacher and Irene were both hugging him.

Where is Dede? Jill thought suddenly. She looked from one face to the other and finally found her at the other end of the gym, being guided backward by her helper. When they got to Jill's end, they picked up a ball and Dede started shooting baskets. She made four out of six.

"I never knew she could do that! She's good!"

"Yes. She's not bad. Considering." Mrs. Atkins looked pleased.

"She's not bad, period!"

The boy with the cup-handle ears stood in front of them.

"Hi, Mrs. Atkins," he said. "How are you today?"

"Just fine, thank you, Donald," Mrs. Atkins said, as if she hadn't spoken to him earlier.

He came to Jill. "Hi. How are you today?"

"Er . . . just fine, thank you, Donald."

Jill sat with Dede and Debbie in the lunchroom and realized she wasn't feeling afraid any more. She felt welcome. More than that. She felt . . . important to them.

"We'll be leaving soon, kids," Mrs. Atkins said.

"I have to sh-show Jill something," Dede said. She coughed harshly.

Mrs. Atkins looked worried. "Don't be long then. I'd like to get you home." She started picking up empty glasses and plates.

"I have to sh-show Jill s-something." Dede pulled Jill out of the room. They went along the corridor and down some stairs to a lower floor.

In a dim storeroom, a row of clay pots stood on a shelf.

"There!" Dede said.

"What are they?"

"Flowers. They're fl-flowers." She sneezed.

"Bless you," Jill said, looking at the pots. They were filled nearly to the top with earth. Poking up out of each one was a rough brown cone, a clumsy dead-looking thing. "Dede . . . are you sure? I mean, they don't look like flowers to me."

"The fl-flowers inside."

"Dede, is anyone . . . helping you with them? I . . . I don't think they're even alive, Dede. Look at them. They're all . . ."

"I'm growing them. J-just me. And n-nobody knows but you. I p-planted them in October. I'm w-watering them and taking c-care of them. I know there's a fl-flower inside."

Fifteen

Jill tramped down the front walk. The New Year's snow squeaked underfoot and the wind tore her breath away. To think there was hot sun shining in California!

Halfway down Dede's block, Jill stopped. An ambulance was standing at the curb. As she watched, two men pulled a stretcher out of the back. They disappeared into the Atkinses' house, while she stood anchored to the sidewalk, feeling sick.

The door opened and the men came out with the stretcher between them.

"Dede!" She began running, her breath coming in painful gasps — running as she had once before, that hot summer afternoon.

Dede was strapped in a cocoon of blankets.

Her eyes were glittering and her face shone with perspiration. But she wasn't silent like Mrs. Lacey. She was breathing — short, sharp little breaths, each one ending in a dull grunt, as if she was using all her strength to push the last bit of air out of her body.

"You a friend of hers?" asked the man in front.

"Yes," Jill whispered. "She just had a cold. What happened? What's the matter with her?"

"Pneumonia."

Mrs. Atkins came down the steps carrying an overnight bag. "Jill!"

"Mrs. Atkins, I thought she just had a bad cold. She was better yesterday — better than when I saw her Friday! Is it really pneumonia?"

"Yes. It's happened before. Once she gets a cold . . ." Mrs. Atkins shook her head. "She just doesn't have any resistance."

"Let's go, ma'am," the man said.

Mrs. Atkins climbed into the back of the ambulance and he began to close the doors.

"Mrs. Atkins!"

"What, honey?"

"Tell her . . . tell her I . . . I'll take care of Barney for her."

The ambulance drove away. Jill watched it go around the corner onto Main and then she turned homeward. I'll walk Barney later, she thought. Maybe by that time Mrs. Atkins'll know how long Dede has to stay in the hospital . . . Dede will be scared being there. She won't know why she has to stay. Will she remember it from the times before? Jill could picture her lying pale on a pillow, with tubes and an oxygen tent, the way it looked on TV. She passed Mrs. Lacey's house. The gate was banging in the cold wind. Some people from New York City had bought the place, but they hadn't moved in yet. Jill shivered as she latched the gate shut. She started running.

"Rose Bowl's next," Larry was saying as she ran into the house.

"How can you stand watching so much football?" Jill said.

"I've got a bet on the Rose Bowl. I'm giving Rusty five points on Washington."

"What do you mean?"

"Michigan's the favorite, dummy. So I'm saying Michigan's going to win by more than five points. If they don't, I'm out a buck."

"What a way to spend New Year's Day!" Jill went to the fire to warm her hands. "Dede's in the hospital, Mom."

"No!"

"She has pneumonia. The ambulance came just as I got there. Pneumonia's serious, isn't it?"

Dad said, "It's an inflammation of the lungs. Mrs. Atkins must be worried."

"She is. She says Dede's had it before. How long do you think she'll have to be in the hospital?"

"A week at least, maybe longer in her case," Mom said.

The Cotton Bowl ended and the Rose Bowl began. Warm again, Jill watched the firelight gleaming on the Christmas ornaments.

"Look at your mother." Dad smiled.

Mom had dropped off to sleep in her chair, the baby bulging into her lap. She'd taken to napping off and on during the day.

"It's like she's switching into a dream life far away from the rest of us," Dad said. "She's all bound up with that life inside her now."

They nodded.

"I want you kids to help your mother all you can. She's pretty uncomfortable at this point and getting ready for the holidays kind of took it out of her. And you know, waiting for this baby is quite a strain on her."

"We'll pitch in, Dad," Tom said.

"I can do all the cleaning," Larry said. "I'm getting my system down pretty good."

"Don't worry," Jill said. "We'll take care of her. Everything's going to turn out okay." She was as sure of that baby as Dede was of her flowers, curled up in the dark and growing toward the light.

Jill stared into the fire, thinking about Dede.

"Dad," she said at last, "I want to ask you a favor."

He spread his arms wide. "Ask me anything!"

Jill told him about the hidden bulbs. "Dede's so sure they're going to flower. But they won't, because she won't be there to water them . . . Dad, I want to go to Pearson tomorrow to get them."

"Well . . . hold on now . . . We'll be kind of busy after the holiday . . ."

"You could do it in your lunch hour. I've just figured it out. I get out of Social Studies at eleven-seventeen, and I don't have another class until twelve because of lunch and recess. We can make it. You'll just have to give me a note . . . What do you think?"

"I think you've a talent for organization, that's what!"

Tuesday morning the air was like crystal. Jill ran down her steps just as Karen came up the street.

"Hey, Karen! Did you have a good time at your cousin's?"

"Fantastic! There were eight of us kids there the whole week and we skated every day. I've gotten really good. Look, there's Marla."

"Oh-oh. She must've come home last night."

"She did. She called me. Hi, Marla."

"Hi, Karen," Marla said.

Jill smiled. "Hi, Marla."

"Hi."

"I didn't know you were back."

"I called my friends."

"Oh. Say, listen, Marla, I really am sorry I had to miss your show . . . Karen and Connie told me you were . . . fabulous."

"You don't have to say that. I got the picture. You had more important things to do."

"Marla . . . I explained all that in my Christmas card."

"Really? Did you send me a Christmas card?"

"You know I did. A ballerina dancing near a Christmas tree."

"I may have seen it. It's hard to remember one particular card. I've been getting such a lot of mail. Karen, didn't we have an absolutely fabulous time?"

"Yes . . . fabulous." Karen looked uncomfortable.

Jill tried again. "I told you I couldn't help it."

"Sure. As my grandma said at the time, it was your loss, not mine! Come on, Karen."

Jill let them go.

At eleven-thirty the car headed up the hill to Pearson.

"I'll wait outside for you, Jilly."

"Dad, you have to come in with me," Jill said. "They'll pay more attention to me if you're

140

there. Anyway, I can't carry all the pots by my-self. I think there were six."

"Well, okay."

"What's the matter?"

"It's just . . . I've never been in a place like that before . . ."

Jill grinned. "You'll do just fine, Dad. Just fine!"

At the desk, they asked for Mrs. Linner.

"She's on her lunch break. I'll see if I can find her," the receptionist said. They waited by the desk.

"Hi. How are you today?" a deep, slow voice said.

Dad turned. "Oh . . . er . . . um . . ."

Jill said, "Just fine, thank you, Donald. How are you today?"

"Just fine, thank you." Donald walked on down the hall.

"Say, Jilly. You seemed right at home with that boy."

"I know him. That's what it takes."

In a moment, Mrs. Linner appeared. "Yes?"

"I'm Jill Harvey and this is my dad. We're friends of Dede Atkins."

"Yes?"

"Well . . . You know Dede's in the hospital and she's been growing some flowers here at school and . . . and we came to pick them up.

She might miss seeing them bloom if she's out of school for a while."

"I'm afraid you're mistaken, Jill. We're not growing anything at present. We'll be doing that in the spring."

"*She* is. She's been doing it by herself. She didn't tell anyone. But she showed them to me at the Christmas party. I know where they are."

"My goodness — by herself? How did she . . ." Mrs. Linner smiled. "Well, you'd better show me their hiding place."

Down in the storeroom, the pots stood in their peaceful twilight.

"I can't see," Mrs. Linner said, and switched on the light.

Jill flinched from the glare and then ran to the bulbs. "She did it! Look at them! Oh, I'm so glad we came, Dad!"

The bulbs had broken open. Pale green tips reached up toward the light from five out of the six brown shells.

"I'm amazed she was able to carry out this project on her own. She had no help whatsoever?" Mrs. Linner asked.

"No."

"Wonderful We have noticed she's gained confidence in the last few months. She has made great strides."

They carried the pots upstairs.

"Hi, babe!" Debbie was standing by the desk.

"Hi, Debbie," Jill said.

"Wh-what you got?"

"Dede's flowers."

"I don't see no flowers."

"The flowers are inside, Debbie."

On the way home, Dad said, "You get along with those kids, don't you?"

"I guess so. I was even thinking . . . well, maybe next year . . . when I'm in the seventh grade, I might work up there sometimes. They need kids like me to help kids like them."

"That's a nice idea, Jilly."

He speeded up. "I'm due back. We'd better drop these off quickly, then I'll take you on to school."

Jill set down one of the pots and rang Dede's doorbell. No answer. "Mrs. Atkins is out, Dad. Shall I just leave them on the porch?"

"Yes. I'll bring up the others." Dad climbed the porch steps. "She's probably at the hospital. Why don't you leave a note?" He pulled a pencil and an old envelope out of his pocket.

Jill took them and wrote: *Mrs. Atkins, these are some flowers Dede was growing at Pearson. Maybe you could take one to the hospital to make her feel better. She's been waiting for them to bloom. Love, Jill.*

Sixteen

Jill jogged all the way home from school. It's a good way to keep warm, she thought. And I won't have to listen to Marla. She let herself in the house quietly, in case Mom was napping.

"Jilly! Thank goodness you're home!" Mom stood at the top of the stairs. Her face was white.

"Why? What's the matter?"

"Jill . . ." Mom came down the stairs carefully. "I called your Dad. But he's out of the office. Honey, I . . . I think the baby's coming."

"The baby? But . . . it's not February . . . it can't . . . it's not time yet!"

"I know. But I know the signs." She clutched Jill's arm. "I'm frightened, Jilly. It's too soon. Oh, I knew something would happen . . ."

"Momma! What should I do? Do you want to lie down? I'll call Dad again . . . No, the doctor! Or the hospital!

When the ambulance came, Jill was throwing Mom's toothbrush and nightdress into a suitcase.

"Did you get through to your father?" Mom was looking lost and scared. "I want him. I want Joe. The baby's too early. It's going all wrong . . ."

"He's still out. They're looking for him. He's in one of the other mills, they think."

"Jilly, I . . ."

Jill put her arm around her. "It's going to be okay, Mom. I have this feeling . . . honest . . . You're going to be fine and the baby's going to be fine . . ."

"I want to think so. But things aren't the way they should be . . . Oh, where's Joe? I don't want to be there alone."

"He'll come. And I'll go with you."

The ambulance men brought in a stretcher and carried Mom out of the house. Jill took the suitcase and climbed in the back and they pulled away. She remembered the driver. He had come for Dede.

"Hold on, little momma," the other man said. "We'll get you there in time."

It was the smoothest ride she'd ever had, but at even the tiniest bump in the road, Mom

145

winced. It seemed to take forever — the baby working away to be born and all of them willing it to hold back. But, finally, the ambulance slid up to the emergency entrance and they whisked Mom inside.

"Tell them at the desk we've taken her right up," the man said to Jill.

At the desk, the nurse said angrily, "They had no business taking her up without going through admitting." She glared at Jill.

"They were in a big hurry," Jill apologized. "Can I take her suitcase to her? Do you know which room she'll be in?"

"I'm assigning her to Room 702, Obstetrics. But you can't go up. Against regulations. I'll have an aide take the suitcase." The nurse stared down at her. "How old are you? How come you're here alone? Where's your father?"

"I'm twelve. And he's coming . . . I hope . . ."

"Well, you can wait in the lobby. That way you'll see him when he comes in," the nurse said. "There are some magazines. Don't worry. Your mom will be fine! Babies are born every day!"

What did she know? She didn't know anything about Mom. Or that other baby. . .

Jill trailed into the lobby and sat on a vinyl chair with hard metal arms. She flipped through a magazine. She didn't see the pages. She looked at the shiny floor and the shiny chairs and the shiny tables. She had to go to the bathroom, but she didn't dare leave her chair in case she missed Dad. She checked the clock. Two hours had gone by. She stared at the wall.

"Jill! What are you doing here?" She jumped. Mrs. Atkins sat down beside her. "You know, they won't let you see Dede, honey."

She'd forgotten Dede was upstairs somewhere, too.

"I'm waiting for my Dad. Mom's here."

"Not the baby? But I thought . . ."

"It's early, Mrs. Atkins. That's bad, isn't it?"

Jill could see Mrs. Atkins didn't want to admit it. She patted Jill's arm. "Oh, not dangerously early, honey," she said. "What is it? Three weeks, maybe? A month? Of course . . . it'd be better if it had waited . . ."

Jill stiffened. "It's six weeks early."

Mrs. Atkins said quickly, "Six weeks? That's nothing. All I meant was . . . well, the baby would be just a bit bigger and stronger . . . but I'm sure it'll be okay. Lots of babies come early . . . they don't read the books!"

Jill tried to smile. "Uh . . . how's Dede? I left something for her on your porch."

"That's nice of you, honey." She frowned. "This is the third time she's had pneumonia. I try to be careful — keep her wrapped up and all — but she's so delicate . . ."

That seemed weird, calling Dede delicate.

Mrs. Atkins went on. "You know, kids who have Down's syndrome used to die young, taken off by pneumonia or other illnesses — they just couldn't resist infection. But nowadays, thank God, with antibiotics, they come through." She lit a cigarette. Jill noticed her hand was shaking. "All the same, it's tough on them — tougher each time. Dede's lungs have been damaged and this climate is wearing her down." She leaned back and closed her eyes. "I've got to take her away. Somewhere warm, dry."

"A vacation would do her good."

"I don't mean a vacation. I mean — move."

Jill stared. "Leave here for good?"

Mrs. Atkins opened her eyes and sat forward. "That's right. I've made up my mind. I'm going to pack up and take her to Arizona just as soon as she's well enough to go. We can stay at my mother's place till we find a place of our own. She'll do better in the sun there . . ."

"But . . . how can you just go like that?"

"I can. It's only a question of doing it. I've put it off too long already and Dede's health has suffered. You see, I always sort of hoped Dede's dad would come walking back through our door one day — figured if I stayed put, then he'd know where to come if he wanted to." She blew her nose. "And then . . . well, I always thought it'd be hard on Dede, moving, having to start all over again in a new place, a new school, trying to find friends. She has a happy life here. Her teachers are fine people and they've taught her so much and then you came along and she loves you. . ."

Jill couldn't say anything. It was too sudden. She felt mixed up. Sure, it'd be good for Dede. But Dede would miss her. And she'd miss Dede, too. And old Barney, Squeak's buddy.

"Jilly!" Dad ran across the lobby. "What happened? Is Mom okay?"

"I don't know. They took her up ages ago."

He hurried over to the desk.

Mrs. Atkins said, "I'll be on my way home now your Dad is here. Do you want to come home with me?"

Jill shook her head.

Mrs. Atkins said, "Call me if you need anything, Jill." She touched her shoulder and left.

Jill sat tense in her chair, her eyes fixed on Dad. The nurse had picked up the phone. After a moment, she put it down and he leaned forward. Then his shoulders slumped.

It can't be! It's not fair! Jill remembered the sturdy little thumps against her hand long ago. I don't believe it, she thought. She ran to her father.

Dad turned slowly and there were tears running down his cheeks. "Jilly!" He choked and held her tight. "Oh, Jilly."

"But I was so sure!"

He held her away from him. "No, Jilly! No! You were right! Don't they always say faith moves mountains? They're both *okay*!"

Seventeen

Barney barked his deep welcome as Jill stamped the snow off her boots.

"Your jacket's really wet, Jill," Mrs. Atkins said. "Can you stay a minute? I'll hang it in the laundry room to dry." She looked out at the falling snow. "That's spring snow, isn't it? Halfway rain, now we're halfway through February." She led Jill into the den. "I'll get back to work. The house is on the market, you know, and I think I've got a buyer. I've been packing up the books and the good china. We'll be out in that Arizona sunshine pretty soon, won't we, Dede?"

"Yeh." Dede coughed.

"Are you feeling better today, Dede?" Jill asked.

"Yeh." Dede smiled, but she looked very tired.

"What do you want to do?" Jill asked.

"I don't know."

"We could watch TV if you like . . . or make some cookies. . ."

"Yeh."

"Hey — how are your bulbs doing?"

Dede's face brightened. "I'll sh-show you." She led the way upstairs.

"Dede!" Jill gasped as they came into Dede's bedroom. The bulbs were ranged along the windowsill, a blaze of pink and white and blue. The whole room was filled with cool fragrance.

"What are they?" Jill asked.

"They're fl-flowers."

"What kind?"

"Hyacinths," Mrs. Atkins said, coming into the room behind them. "Dede must've found them in the toolshed. I was planning to plant them last fall but I forgot all about them."

"They took such a long time to bloom, though," Jill said. "October to February. I don't know if I could wait that long."

"They're s-slow," Dede said. "The fl-flower's inside."

Mrs. Atkins smiled at Dede. "Some things are worth waiting for, aren't they?"

* * *

Jill worked the baby carriage carefully along the sidewalk. The wheels balked every now and then in the slush, but the baby slept on, snuggled under her blankets. Thin March sunshine gleamed through the bare branches of the maple trees and lit up the fluff of red on Faith's head. Jill leaned down to touch her every now and then — make sure she was breathing. She couldn't explain how she felt — people would probably laugh at her if they knew — but it filled her with awe that they'd been given a living, working baby, and that something so small could be so complete, that each tiny finger had a tiny fingernail, that the hair was growing, and the delicate fan of lashes shaded eyes that cried and smiled and turned to watch the world around her.

Squeak trotted beside them, pulling harder as they got closer to Dede's. The moving truck was already parked outside. Jill stopped the baby carriage and watched the procession of things disappearing through the gaping doors at the back. Dede was nowhere around. She still had to stay indoors.

Karen's brother John got off his bike to watch the movers. So did some other kids, filling time this Easter vacation. Mrs. Cohen paused with her bag of groceries. And a couple of women Jill had never even seen before. They all stood there together, staring silently, as if it were a free show staged just for them. Jill suddenly felt like an intruder, spying on Dede's private life, and she turned the baby carriage abruptly homeward.

A chilly wind chased clouds across the sun and a spray of snow hit her face as she carried Faith inside. Mom was singing in the kitchen. She just about never stopped these days.

Jill didn't feel happy and she didn't want to be with someone who was. She put Faith in her crib and then stretched out on her bed and stared at the snow beginning again, driven by the wind that was driving Dede away. In a few hours, Dede's house would be as empty as Mrs. Lacey's and Dede just as surely gone out of her life. Funny I should feel so bad about it now, she thought. In the beginning, she hadn't even wanted to know Dede and, in lots of ways, things would be easier without her around. So why did she have this empty feeling inside?

She tried to read, but she couldn't. Faith stirred in her crib and began to cry. Jill went in and picked her up, cradling her against her shoulder. She held her long after she'd stopped crying. Nestling the baby against her, she walked to the window. In a while, the snow out there would be gone and flowers would start pushing through the muddy ground. Mrs. Atkins said Dede could grow a garden full in Arizona. That would make her happy. But would she find someone to show them to? Or would the kids in Arizona make fun of her and tease her and after a while ignore her so they wouldn't have to be bothered with her? She turned from the window and held Faith closer.

She heard the doorbell ring. Mom called up the stairs. "Come down, Jilly. Dede and her mother are here to say goodbye."

Everyone stood around smiling and saying all the same old things, like "Have a good trip!" and "Boy, I wish I was going to Arizona!" It was all so stupid. They were just things to say to fill the time till they left. Jill and Dede stood in the middle of all the cheerful talk as if they were alone. Dede didn't seem to understand she wouldn't see Jill again, that she was going away for good. She didn't know what lay ahead of her.

Suddenly, Jill was hugging Dede hard. Words wouldn't come. Dede said, "It's okay. It's okay." She knew what Jill was saying. Goodbye. Take care. I love you.

Jill stood on the sidewalk waving the car out of sight.

Marla came up the block. "Who're you waving at?" she asked.

Jill turned. "Dede. She just left for Arizona."

"Oh, that's right. I heard they were going."

Jill tried to speak lightly around the lump in her throat. "I know it sounds weird . . . but I'm going to miss her."

"No kidding? You really will? You know, I never could figure out why you liked her so much. I mean . . . like, she's pretty strange. You have to admit that. And she doesn't know anything about anything."

There was a silence.

Jill said slowly, "Dede Atkins may never be a ballerina" — then she lifted her chin — "but she knows more about being a friend than anyone else I know."